THE GENERAL'S
WIFE

BETHANY BELLEMIN

Copyright © 2024 Bethany Bellemin.

All rights reserved. No part of this book may be reproduced, stored, or transmitted by any means—whether auditory, graphic, mechanical, or electronic—without written permission of both publisher and author, except in the case of brief excerpts used in critical articles and reviews. Unauthorized reproduction of any part of this work is illegal and is punishable by law.

ISBN: 979-8-89031-931-9 (sc)
ISBN: 979-8-89031-932-6 (hc)
ISBN: 979-8-89031-933-3 (e)

Because of the dynamic nature of the Internet, any web addresses or links contained in this book may have changed since publication and may no longer be valid. The views expressed in this work are solely those of the author and do not necessarily reflect the views of the publisher, and the publisher hereby disclaims any responsibility for them.

One Galleria Blvd., Suite 1900, Metairie, LA 70001
(504) 702-6708

CONTENTS

Meeting 1

Learning Something New 10

Battle Times 17

New Start 21

Beauty before War 27

Schemes and Shadows 32

Pieces and Puzzles 36

Matching of Wits 40

Coming to the Surface 44

Mind Games 48

Beneath a Pale Moon 54

Setting Moons and Rising Suns 58

Is Blood Thicker Than Water? 62

The Stars Align 67

Where Once We Met 73

Until the End of Time 78

To the Final Word 84

From the Author 89

MEETING

"Why did the emperor give you the barbarian woman?" Only Yan Bin could have been so forward with the question. He and Fu Xianning were brothers in arms, and Yan Bin had been his armor-bearer these last ten years.

"I do not know. I suspect it was so he could refuse being entangled in a foreign intrigue. I have no interest in her, it is a mere formality." Xianning finished writing his oracles and stood up from his desk.

"The wedding is tonight. I will meet her and promise her shelter and food for life, but that is all she will receive from me. She is a pawn, even if she doesn't know it."

"I have heard her hair is the color of gold and she refuses to speak to anyone," Yan Bin mused.

Xianning shrugged. "We will have nothing to talk about anyways. Let her refuse my questions. I shall find out why she was given to me."

Two hours later, after the briefest ceremony he could arrange, Xianning entered his room to see the veiled woman who had become his bride. Pulling the veil back revealed startling blue eyes. Her green hairpin contrasted sharply to her gold hair that fell to her knees. She was shaking but held her chin up. Xianning motioned to a chair.

"Please be seated." She hesitated, looking between his pointing hand and the chair, then sat down.

"Who are you?" he asked, getting straight to the point. She shook her head, bewildered. It occurred to Xianning that perhaps she could not understand any Chinese. He asked her a few more questions, but her eyes seemed truthful as she only shook her head. With hand motions, he tried to make it clear she would go to her own pavilion and stay there. But it wasn't clear, and she stood up looking about her, wondering what she needed to do. Finally, he roughly took her hand and led her away to a pavilion on the other side of his house. He ordered the servants to tend her and left. It didn't matter about having a wife. He was stuck with a foreign beauty who could not or would not speak to him and perhaps was placed in his household as a spy for the Mongols too.

He did not sleep that night. Was there a mole in the emperor's court, and now the Mongol chief would know that she was living with one of the head generals battling the Western invasion? Was it all a plot to report his movements back to betray him to his archnemesis? He clenched his fist and smiled grimly. He would not be so easily fooled.

The next several days he gave very little thought to his new wife, until a week later. He was crossing the courtyard and saw his old nurse carrying a tray of food. His wife walked toward her and received the tray with a smile and bow. This was a queer situation. Why should she bow to a servant? Though he himself reverenced his old nurse, why would this strange woman do so? He frowned and proceeded on with his day.

The afternoon brought Yan Bin with grim news from a courier. Luck was against the Chinese forces, it seemed, and the invaders had come even further into the kingdom. Xianning immediately began writing to his generals. He felt frustrated at being homebound as the emperor had ordered him back for a full month to marry and enjoy his new bride. He felt the waste of time might cost them irreparable losses.

"Has she spoken to you yet?" Yan Bin asked as he stood at the door staring into the courtyard, his hands clasped behind his back, watching the courier who stood by the gate, ever on alert.

"No. I suspect she does not know our language. But no matter. If she cannot understand us, then she cannot spy on us either."

"You don't suppose she's simply pretending not to understand?"

"I have wondered at it. Before I leave for the battlefront, I will make sure."

The next two weeks went by quickly, and he was soon preparing to leave. He did not anticipate returning before winter some ten months away at least.

He executed his plan with his usual finesse. He ordered his wife to be brought to his pavilion. As she stood silently before him, he waited until she would see the snake. A harmless snake of course. He had released it just moments before she arrived. Fear would make her speak. She did see the snake. And she did cry out. But it was a silent scream, no sound escaped her lips. She climbed atop a chair, pointing and gesturing as though she was telling him to beware of danger. But all was in silent pantomime. He ordered Yan Bin to retrieve the pest and approached her. She still stood on the chair, her hair fluttering about her frightened face. Why hadn't she at least screamed aloud? He glanced over at his old nurse, Qing Shan, who had accompanied her mistress.

"Why is she so silent?"

"My lord, I have watched her for three weeks, and she has not uttered a single sound. I fear she is mute."

He looked back at the young woman's face and thought that somehow this might be the answer after all. One last chance, though, before he left to be sure. He helped her down from the chair, and as she turned to walk away, he grabbed her hand and spun her toward him. She stumbled, her mouth open and still silent. He caught her fall and released her, refusing to look at the startled face. He felt a twinge of regret to have frightened her so badly. It must indeed be true that she was mute. She should have made some noise and yet here she stood, quiet and frightened.

"Qing Shan, I am leaving tomorrow morning. Make sure she is well fed, clothed, and as content as you can make her. I doubt she wants to be here anymore than I want her. I do not need to see her again. Have a doctor see if her silence can be cured. Let her lack nothing, but do not bother me with her either." The next morning, he was gone.

Those next few months were long and bitter. Many battles were fought, some won and some lost.

Xianning's chance to turn the tide came one frosty morning. Two powerful armies clashed with China's youngest general in the lead. His horse was killed shortly after the fray began. Falling from the crashing beast, Xianning rolled to his feet, kicking away a spear that thrust toward him. Each opponent he crossed seemed stronger than the last, or was he just feeling weaker? Then he came face to face with Muqali himself, leader of the northern Mongolian army that had been warring against them for so long. They battled fiercely, almost oblivious to others around them. The frosty ground had turned muddy, and they slid about with swords flashing in the cold autumn sun. Xianning suddenly felt a burning in his shoulder, then another pain shot to his back. The flaring pains made him realize he had been struck by two arrows. He fought on, but Muqali's face was a blur before him. He heard someone shouting for General Fu. He remembered falling with one last sword thrust at the sneering face of his enemy. Then he remembered no more.

When he awoke, he was in his field bed, covered in bloody bandages. Yan Bin was standing beside him, his shoulder and right arm wrapped in bandages. A long cut crossed his face, and he seemed to have aged three years. Seeing his general awake, he shouted for the physician and dropped to his knees beside the cot.

"Sir, you're awake! That is good, I thought I had lost my leader. We saw you fall and made a rush to bring your body back. We feared we had only succeeded for your burial." A tear slid down his nose, and Xianning smiled at him. "I won't die so easily."

Once again Xianning found himself recalled home by the emperor, though this time due to his wounds received in battle. The emperor, it seemed, was intent on making sure his youngest general lived a long life. Back home, he was busy with affairs of war, and it was nearly ten days before he asked how his wife was. Qing Shan reported that doctors had confirmed her as a permanent mute, though a healthy person. Xianning thought that the emperor wished to rid himself of a burden by his supposed gift. Now Xianning had to deal with her, though he held nothing against her for what most would consider an ailment. Xianning was a hard man, but not so base as that.

It was by complete accident that the next morning he caught sight of his wife. Walking past a room, he saw her cleaning, her hair twisted into a long rope of gold to stay out of her way. She was so intent on her work that she apparently had not heeded him passing by the door. He was surprised to find her working as if she were part of the household staff and slipped behind a shadowed tapestry to see what this was about. Qing Shan entered at that moment, followed by lady Ran, head housekeeper of his mansion.

Ran slapped the food out of the nanny's hand, screaming, *"How could you feed that barbarian trash?* No more food from my kitchen goes to her, I've told you many times! Let her go beg in the streets. Even the general can't stand the sight of her, why should we tolerate her presence?" Without hesitation, and to Xianning's shock, his wife crossed the room and began cleaning up the mess. Ran kicked at her savagely. This was too much for the lord of the house. He emerged from his hiding spot and all three women froze.

"I will have you flogged for this, Ran! Whatever she may be by birth, she is also my wife! Both of you, leave now!" The maids scurried away, and his wife stood up, turning to face him. The broken bowl had cut her finger, and a drop of blood spattered to the floor. He took her hand and wrapped it in his sash. He noticed there were scars on her wrist. He wondered to himself about it and motioned for her to follow him to his desk.

"I know you don't understand me, but you mustn't let the servants behave that way toward you. I don't even know your name but..." He stopped. She was nodding and smiling. Could she understand after all? He decided to test her. He pointed toward his shelf. "Bring me the blue vase." She promptly did so and set it gracefully down on his desk. He frowned a little. How long had she understood Chinese?

He then ordered her to retrieve a stack of letters. To his amazement, she organized them by date before placing the stack before him. His fist crashed to the table. She jumped as he stood up. "You have been lying ignorance of our language. How long have you understood?" She held up two fingers.

"Two weeks?"

She shook her head no. "Two months!"

She nodded and smiled. She gestured toward his inkwell, and he pushed it toward her with a blank page. She seated herself across from him and began writing. Her penmanship was rather remarkable for being new to the language, and he felt his wariness increase. After a moment, she handed the paper back to him. He read her words with mixed thoughts.

I am sorry I could not speak to you before. My tongue is still, but my ears are quick. I learn languages very fast. Qing Shan has helped me learn to write as well. But your language has challenged me greatly and I still have much to learn.

He looked back at her. For the first time, he wondered what her name was.

"What is your name?" His sharp voice was followed by the scratching of the feather pen as she took a new page and began writing. She hesitated a few times, seeming to try to remember the correct words to translate to him.

My name has been changed many times. I was born as Brenna. But you may change my name to suit you as you wish.

He thought for a moment and stared at her unflinching eyes. Was she just bold, or was she a menace?

"Why have you had so many names?"

Her pen responded, *My story is long.*

He frowned; she was evading his question now.

"Write it all down. I will return this evening." He pushed a stack of papers to her and left.

He went out to the village and walked about aimlessly, his thoughts split between the war and the enigma he called his wife. Hours went by while he wandered. Finally, he returned to find her head resting on the desk. She was asleep. The stack of papers had writing on them now. He quietly slid the pages away and sat down in the corner to read. As he read, his curiosity and interest grew stronger.

I was born in a castle in the country of England. It is very far west from here. My mother died at my birth, and I was raised by a holy man. The holy man is called a friar there, and he taught me to read and write. Women are not supposed to be clerics in that world, I always kept my knowledge secret. I was taken away by a wealthy man's wife who thought I would amuse her. We went to another country called France where she had her second castle. She sold me to her brother's household when I was ten. He was going on a crusade to the Middle East, and I was brought along to be the cook's help. It was a very long journey to Jerusalem. Three years, in fact, before we reached it, for we stopped in both Greece and again in Constantinople. Jerusalem was flooded in war, and I was taken away with other children by Muslim raiders. We were to be traded at a great sheikh's house. The sheikh had a wondrous horse, but he could not tame it. In an angry fit, the sheikh declared that whoever could ride his stallion would become his heir. I sneaked in with the horse that night and befriended it. Perhaps, because I cannot speak, he sensed a companion. For three nights I sneaked in and stayed with the stallion secretly. The third day I rode him before the master, and the sheikh kept his word. I was taken in as his daughter. My life there was not bad. I had always been at best a servant and at worst a slave. It was strange to adjust. I learned Persian in my three years with him. We went to India during this time to trade goods. My Arab father was very wealthy. We were there a year, and I learned some of the Sanskrit language, which helped him with his trades. He was very pleased with me but unexpectedly he died one morning. I cried for the first time. His wives had never liked me, and I was immediately sold to slave traders. We came walking behind a trail of camels for a long time. Those were my worst days, I think. The lands we came through took many, many months of travel, and not all of the slaves survived. Finally, we stopped at a trading town. A Mongol chieftain came to buy and saw me. I was purchased and brought to China. I learned some Mongolian speech at this time just by listening to my captors. I do not know why he dressed me in finery and sent me to your emperor. His highness, the emperor, was very displeased at seeing me. I do not know what he said, but somehow, I came here to be given to you. My journey has been long, I can understand and write fairly well in five languages because of this. If you wish to send me away too, please let me first say goodbye to Qing Shan. She is my first friend and has taught me the customs of your country. I could not bear to lose my first friend. I hope you understand my words and are not displeased with me. I have no control over my past life, but I always try to make my future honorable.

He stood up and walked over to the sleeping form. He felt unsure as to his next step. Was it possible for one person to have gone through so much and traveled so far? The scars on her wrist seemed to match some of her story. Whatever the case, she felt truthful, but he needed to know why Muqali had sent her to the emperor. He would set his spies to finding out. He had not been curious about his wife before, and now he felt he could think of nothing else. Annoyed with himself, he picked her up and took her to the next room to lay her on the couch to sleep more comfortably. She awoke at the movement and struggled to be put down. He placed her firmly on the chair and did not look at her again as he walked away. He felt, rather than saw, her frustrated face.

He somehow knew that she was thinking he didn't believe her. He wasn't sure if he did or not. It seemed too fantastical to be true, yet her story also seemed too fantastical to be made up. Whatever it was, he would verify what he could.

LEARNING SOMETHING NEW

Xianning was busy writing at his desk, forcing himself to think of anything other than his wife's past. He had refused to see her at all for a month now. He knew she might be anxious about what he planned to do with her, but until he had answers he could not know what he planned to do himself. As it turned out, Yan Bin had some answers today.

"We traced her story to her capture of the Mongols. She was bought from a camel train. And she had traveled from India." So that much was true. Xianning marveled she had survived the slave train. Many did not. He dismissed Yan Bin and continued his work.

His wounds hurt today, perhaps the weather was changing. He rubbed his shoulder and clenched his fist, wondering about how soon he could return to the war. Wounds were far better than clerical pains. He wasn't sure how long she had stood there, but he felt rather than heard a sound and, looking up, he saw his wife standing in the doorway, holding a tray.

"Yes?" he asked gruffly. She bowed and came forward offering him tea.

"You may pour it," he responded and was amazed at how perfectly she performed the task with the traditional ways of any Chinese wife. She was a fast learner, almost frighteningly fast. When she finished, he dismissed her, but she did not leave.

"What is it?" He asked pushing ink and paper toward her. She wrote, *If your wounds ail you, I can write for you as you dictate. I have done such work before for my Arab father. And I have been studying your language every day. I believe I can assist well enough.*"

He was about to refuse, but then he thought of the mound of writing left to do, and his shoulder (while he would never admit it) hurt worse when he wrote.

"You may begin then. I hope you write quickly."

She did write quickly, and the day was waning when at last he said to stop. She looked up, her face tired but her eyes alive. She was glad to have such work. Probably she had so often been bored as a mere servant. He dismissed her and she bowed her way out.

He didn't sleep much that night. He thought about his wife's past and those scars on her wrist. And he felt sorry for her pain, and he was proud of her will to live. And he again thought of what tricks the Mongol chief was up to, and if his court enemy was involved in any way.

The next morning, he called Qing Shan to see him.

"Is there anything you have noticed about your mistress? Behaviors, aspects, anything unusual?"

Qing Shan smiled. "She is quite industrious and strangely gracious to everyone, even to the servants that despise her. She seems to embrace our culture with a rare affinity. She has even begun to learn embroidery and promises to be quite a talent." She seemed ready to say more but hesitated.

"Continue," he ordered.

"You know she has scars on her wrist, but she also has scars on her ankles that appear to be from old burns. Smaller spots at varying degrees of places. As if she was burned on different occasions."

Now this was strange. He thought on this for a moment. "Send her to me."

A few moments later his wife appeared with her silent approach. He frowned; she was almost as quiet as a cat. Why was everything about her so suspicious? He walked around his desk and stood in front of her to see her reaction.

"Why are your ankles burned?" he asked brusquely. She turned scarlet and looked down.

"I'm your husband. If I wish to discuss your ankles, I have that privilege." He pointed to the chair at his desk. "Write it down," he ordered. He felt her embarrassment as she inscribed her answer. She handed it to him without looking in his direction.

When I worked for my French master, I was an assistant to the cook. If the cook was in a bad temper, he would throw hot water at my feet. Her face grew redder as he saw her last note. *Does this make me so ugly to you?*

He stepped beside her and lifted her chin to force her to meet his gaze.

"I do not think of people in terms of appearances, I only consider accomplishments. Now begin writing for me, I have much work to do."

Another day passed and this time, when evening approached, he kept her with him for dinner.

He did not speak the entire meal as he watched her with her new skill at chopsticks. How could she learn things so quickly? He could tell his stares made her uncomfortable, but he rather liked her discomfort.

Perhaps any trap she was planning would reveal itself. Her dress and hair were completely Chinese, despite her obvious variance in hair color and complexion, Qing Shan was right that his wife had adapted to his culture with surprising ease. Even her mannerisms were becoming more Asian and less foreign.

How was it so natural for her to embrace a new life so easily?

The rest of the week went by, and she did many documents for him. He was careful to not let her see any pertinent information, and he would not let Yan Bin report in front of her. She was not offended and would leave at the armor bearer's approach.

Late one night, after working a long day, Xianning awoke to a sound. He knew it was not a usual sound at this time of night. What he had heard was a shutter window click. He slithered out of his blankets and drew a knife that hung above his pillow. A shadow seemed to move outside, and he crept to the doorway. The next moment a man made a loud grunt and a vase crashed to the floor. He ran to the next room and saw his wife thrown back by an assailant. Xianning threw himself at the intruder and for a moment he wasn't sure if he would win. The intruder was a master in the martial arts. But then so was he. At last, Xianning found himself the victor and saw the noise of the fight had awakened the house. He ordered the guards to be doubled and had Yan Bin lock up his new foe. He would have him thoroughly interrogated in the morning.

Qing Shan was helping his wife walk back to her pavilion, but Xianning wasn't done with her yet. He grabbed her shoulder, so she spun around to face him.

"How did you know he was coming?" he thundered. "And why were you in my pavilion?"

She was very pale and shook her head with many hand motions.

Qing Shan came to her aid. "Sir, she is tired and frightened. Could she attend to this tomorrow?"

With a dark look, he agreed.

At sunrise, his wife knocked on his study door. "Enter and write," he demanded. Her story was not quite what he expected.

I heard a noise, a footstep. It was not a familiar footstep outside my pavilion. When I looked out, I saw a shadow skirting the courtyard to your room. I cannot shout to alert the guards. I went to stop him. I'm sorry he was too strong for me, and the vase did not incapacitate him. He read it twice then looked at her.

"How can you identify the sound of an unfamiliar footprint?"

She shrugged and wrote, *Every house I have ever lived in it is the same. I recognize the sound of steps that the household members make. I know a strange step when I hear it.*

He made her sit in the chair across from his desk and pondered this as he worked. He wasn't sure why she would risk her safety for him. Unless she was trying to fool him and gain his confidence.

That night he told her to return to her pavilion and not to leave again without his permission. She turned about, her head up and marched to her place. For a reason he could not explain, he wished she would have looked back once.

His head guards had investigated and tortured his assailant, but the man was a pillar of silence.

He determined that he himself would go the next day. But that wasn't meant to be. Yan Bin appeared before him at breakfast. "The assailant has escaped, sir. It's like he vanished into thin air. Someone must have helped him."

Xianning was furious, but after thorough investigation, nothing was to be found. He had the guards punished and had to let the matter drop.

Several days passed, and two unwelcome guests arrived. It was Zhou Song and his wife: two people that had the emperor's ear in one hand and a knife in the other. Xianning knew of the Zhou jealousy at his position in the army. Though he never said it aloud, he considered

Zhou to be a greater threat than the enemy soldiers he faced in battle. Xianning's greeting to the couple was extremely

Hospitable, and while his face smiled, his brain worked. It was not his first run in with the Zhou's.

"We came to see how you have recovered, Fu Xianning. We heard you nearly died in battle a few months back."

Xianning felt this phrase was spoken with disappointment that they were not attending his funeral. He had tea brought to the great porch and made polite conversation with them.

The lady Zhou Daiyu asked him coquettishly if they were to meet his new wife.

"I hear she has hair like summer sun, a large nose, and looks very strange." She piqued with a fan flutter.

"Of course. If her looks are not to your taste, just choose a concubine," Zhou Song remarked as he ate a grape. Xianning looked at the oily face of his rival and made his own remark.

"I have heard that Lord Zhou is as good at choosing concubines as he is at flattering the emperor. Perhaps, sometime, you may teach me your methods of subterfuge." Lord Zhou gave a sly smile, and he toasted Xianning as a draw to the discussion.

Xianning turned to Yan Bin. "Have my wife brought here."

When his wife entered the porch, he took great pleasure in seeing the Zhou's faces. They were shocked by her beauty and Zhou Daiyu's face flamed with jealousy. Xianning could not resist remarking, "Her nose is quite perfect as noses go."

He saw his wife blush prettily, and he thought with amusement as the Zhou's comments were fully understood by his brilliant wife. But they did not know it. He watched his wife pour tea and smile with the grace of any empress. And he almost glowed with pride. If there were not so many unanswered things about her, he could almost have liked her.

When his guests finally left, he told his wife to follow him to the study. "How did you like them?" he asked, watching her with barely a hidden smirk.

Her writing rather clipped to match her mood. *Your friends are always welcomed to your house, of course they are respectable.*

He hid a smile. "They are rude, and as dangerous as a viper." She looked up quickly with a hint of relief on her face. So she didn't have to like them after all. He wasn't sure why, but he was quite sure that's what she was thinking, and a cute blush convinced him it was true.

He sent her back to her place and began packing. He had, earlier that morning, finally received permission to go back to war. It was time for him to see to his soldiers. He had been away far too long.

He was surprised when he left the next morning to see his wife standing in attendance to tell him goodbye. He stopped in front of her for a moment. "You may write, if you feel there is something to tell me. I have had a bell hung by your bed. Ring it if another intruder comes, and do not attend to it yourself. Perhaps when I return, you may greet me hello?" He glanced at her out if the corner of his eye. He saw her eyelids flutter a little and knew it made her glad.

He had already privately told the servants to attend to her as if she were royalty and never give her trouble again. His order had been *One offense will cost you your tongue. If she cannot speak, at least you should not be able to rail against her.*

He turned away from her and gave orders to his men, then mounting his horse, he refused to look back as he left.

BATTLE TIMES

Xianning was gone for a year. The war was not going well, and though he was wounded several times, none of those injuries were severe enough to take his life. The emperor was displeased, and several severe reprimands had been issued to the generals.

Xianning found himself at night, when his men were mostly asleep, thinking about his wife. She had written him four times in this year. Her letters were merely formality; she was obeying him, but she always signed it *Your Wife*' Why that made him feel warm and cold at the same time, he could not know.

His spies had recovered very little information about her past except to confirm she had lived in the household of a great sheikh some years before. Perhaps it was because he was tired that he had long since stopped suspecting her as an enemy and saw her as only a pawn in the hands of powerful people. He refused to admit he missed her, but sometimes on dark nights with a bitter wind howling outside his tent he rather wished for her. To see her smile and her hair glow in the sun. He wondered why she had dared to attack an assassin on her own. Was she protecting him or herself? If all the things she said about her past were true, there was no end to the things she must have suffered.

He felt himself wondering if she was happy in this new culture or if she missed her foreign lands.

He thought that he would be very grief-filled indeed to never see his homeland again. The world was a dangerous place, especially for a mute woman. Though somehow, he no longer thought of her as mute, more like a pleasant silence that could speak to his mind. If he thought back, there were times he felt by her look that he knew what she would have said if she could speak. Sometimes when pondering this, he smiled, for he saw her irritation with him at moments and guessed what she might have been musing to herself.

The next morning an edict from the emperor arrived. He demanded his top five generals to come to the capital. They were to be reprimanded publicly at best, but of course depending on his mood they might lose their heads. No one could be sure. As they traveled to the capital Xianning had only one regret: he could not see his wife first.

Things were not good at the palace. The emperor raged at them and placed them all under house arrest. For two weeks they were confined to their rooms in the capital with no word on their fate.

Xianning wrote Yan Bin to go home and stay away from the capital. "Who knows if I can keep you safe from the wrath of his highness."

Then one morning they were summoned back to the palace. The emperor smiled cordially to them. "My court favorite has convinced me to save your necks—and to even reward you." The generals glanced at each other in surprise. Then Zhou Song walked out. Xianning smiled grimly inside. So his ultimate enemy was still court favorite.

"All of you are free to return home, because of Zhou Song's elegance. Xianning, remain. I have something to say." After the others had left, the emperor commanded him to stand in front of the throne.

"How do you like the barbarian woman I gave you?"

It was a question Xianning had not anticipated.

"I like her very much," he responded cautiously.

"It was Zhou Song's idea. He said she would suit your tastes. Seems he found her in a slave market, but remember some empresses began lives as brothel attendants, so it really isn't stooping too low to be married to her." A light began to dawn for Xianning, and he watched Zhou's face. With a militaristic bow, he thanked the emperor for his kindness and lord Zhou for his consideration.

"Aren't you anxious to return to her?" Zhou asked, his mouth smiling but his eyes malicious.

Xianning's one word answer—"Yes"—was honest. He *was* anxious to return to her.

He journeyed home alone and quickly. So many pieces were fitting in now; Zhou Song was in league with Muqali. Despite having told the emperor he picked the wife himself, Zhou had not seen her before that day when he came to Xianning's house. His wife would have acknowledged if she had seen the man before. She had been chosen by the Mongol chief specifically to be given to Xianning. She was carefully presented to the emperor as a gift from the warring chief, and Zhou had manipulated the emperor to bestow the exotic beauty to his youngest general. No doubt Zhou planned for her to enrapture his mind and cause him to lose focus on the war. Having failed that, he had sent the assassin, but his wife had foiled that plan. Now Zhou had defended him before the palace and was sending him home. What was his scheme now? There was no doubt in his mind now that his wife was merely an instrument and had no involvement in this sinister plan. Zhou's face when he left had put fear in his heart for the safety of his wife. Zhou's words, *Aren't you anxious to return to her?* had him deeply concerned, and his fears grew the closer he came to home.

After days of travel, he was home. The opened gate, the absence of guards, and the deathly quiet were all wrong.

He galloped into the courtyard and saw Yan Bin standing on the porch.

"Sir, I had no word you would return so soon!" he exclaimed running forward, a mixture of anguish and relief on his face.

"What has happened? Where is my wife?" he demanded, springing down from his horse.

"Sir, I have very bad news. She has been taken. Three men came one night. They knew where her room was. Several guards were killed, and Qing Shan was injured as well. Their kung fu was excellent, they slew many of your guards that were trying to protect her. I had gone out to meet with one of your aids. When I returned, she was gone. I blame myself, sir, and take the responsibility. Please punish me." He had dropped to his knees before his master, his face stricken with grief and regret at failing his duty.

Xianning stood stunned as his fears were realized. "When was this?" he demanded.

"One week ago, sir. I have traced them to the western territory, where the invaders occupy our lands."

So Zhou's men traveled even faster than he had.

"Stand, we have work to do," he commanded. Fresh horses were ordered, and he rushed in to visit the old nurse laying frail and pale on her bed.

She sobbed at seeing him. "Oh, sir, my poor lady, I tried to stop them, I have failed her. Please punish me." She tried to rise from her bed but was too weak.

"Qing Shan, I do not blame you, and neither would she. Get better quickly. I'm going to get her back."

Moments later, Xianning and Yan Bin both thundered out of the gate. If Zhou had seen the face of Xianning at that moment, he would have been afraid.

NEW START

Xianning had followed the trail of his stolen wife to a small enemy encampment. This was where the scouts were, ahead of the army that trailed a few days behind. Yan Bin crouched beside him as they spied on the place before them.

"She will be in the great tent in the center of the camp," Xianning observed, narrowing his eyes. "I'll go in and get her, sir." Yan Bin was unfailing in his loyalty.

"No, we will take down two guards and use their uniforms to enter the camp. We both go in." The first stage of the plan went well. Two guards would never see another day. Dressed as Mongolian soldiers, Xianning and Yan Bin entered under a moonless night. Working their way to the center, they waited until a lull had come. Most of the men had gone to sleep, a few were drinking and shouting at a large table. Xianning recognized the leader of the camp sitting at the table: Muqali's favorite young general, Ilchidey. They had clashed in battle before, and both had scars to remember each other by. A very drunk Ilchidey soon pulled away from the table and headed to the tent they were watching.

His sneering face confirmed Xianning's thoughts. His wife was inside.

They worked their way to the back of the tent. Yan Bin kept watch while Xianning began cutting his way through the course fabric. He heard Ilchidey enter. He heard his words too. Xianning spoke Mongolian fluently and the hair rose on his neck. He heard a little sound and knew his wife was shuffling away from the drunk chief. He heard a slap and Ilchidey yelled. A crash sounded, and Xianning was in the tent. His wife was holding an empty scabbard and the Mongol general was approaching her, the left side of his face still red from the slap Xianning's wife had given him. On the ground between them was the sword she had failed to grab. In a moment, the two men were fighting. Ilchidey was so drunk he hardly remembered that he could yell for assistance. When he did yell, surprisingly no one came. A short struggle, and Xianning clubbed him on the back of the head with brass knuckles. The man crumbled, out cold. At another time, Xianning would have finished him off, but this enemy of China right now was only a barrier to be surmounted. Xianning turned to his wife. Her lip was bleeding, and the look of relief on her face melted his heart.

He wrapped her in his cloak and picked her up. Rejoining Yan Bin, they moved with the shadows.

Yan Bin had set a plan in motion while Xianning was in the tent. A smoke that caused drowsiness had been released near the tent. The guards crouched about limply. Yan Bin held a rag to his nose and offered similar mask to Xianning and his wife. But the toxin only worked for a few moments. Yan Bin had set another plan to work as extra caution. The horse gate was lined with a string of slow burning fireworks. In a moment, they went off and the camp was chasing after the escaping horses. Two guards saw the escapees, and Yan Bin sent them to the grave. Once they had reached their own horses, tied up in a nearby tangled mass of thorns, they took off with the wind. A smattering of arrows followed, but they were away now, and none of the soldiers had a horse to follow with.

When they had ridden miles away, Xianning slowed his mount to a walk. "We will find shelter and rest the horses for two hours, then we will continue."

They reached a suitable place and dismounted. He helped his wife down, and she sank to the ground exhausted. Yan Bin handed provisions to them, and they all sat, eating in silence. For the first time, Xianning really looked at his wife. Her feet were bare, and he saw the scarred ankles. Her face was weary but still so beautiful. He looked at her scarred wrists and her bleeding lip. He swore to himself he would never let her feel pain or fear again. His wife saw him staring at her feet and, blushing, tucked them under her dress. He smiled a little and told her and Yan Bin to rest, he would keep watch.

The next morning saw them many miles from their resting place. And the dawn's light showed something else: Yan Bin had been struck by an arrow the night before. He had said nothing and broke the shaft off, but the broken bit stuck out of his shoulder. It was a deep wound, and they had many days before they would reach a village where they could get help.

Yan Bin was made of granite. Four days later they were safe, out of the Mongols' conquered territory and in a village inn where a local physician was staying. And Yan Bin had survived the wound. While Yan Bin recovered, Xianning had time to talk with his wife.

"How long were you there?" he asked as they sat beside a small river that flowed below the village. She tossed flower petals into the water and motioned with her hands. *Two nights.*

"Did they hurt you much?"

She shook head. By her hand motions and attempts to write in the dirt, it seemed she had traveled rapidly from camp to camp until she came to this last stronghold. Zhou must have planned all along to give her to Ilchidey in revenge against Xianning. She had spent one night alone in the camp, then Ilchidey had come back to camp the second night. Xianning had arrived in time.

She wrote, *I was so glad to see you,* then looked away, a mixture of relief and embarrassment in her expression.

He pulled her face toward him and smiled into her eyes. "I was even more glad to see you. I was thinking of giving you a new name, so the world knows you are my wife."

She smiled and stared down at the flowers in her lap.

"How does Jia Yi sound to you? Fu Jia Yi, my wonderful, beautiful, and brave wife."

Things were very different between them after this. Yan Bin was soon better, nothing held him back for long, and they completed their journey home. Xianning knew that once Zhou heard they had lived through the rescue attempt he would try a new plan, and Xianning would not let himself be caught unawares again.

When they finally arrived home, the house echoed with joy. Even the servants who had not liked her bowed to kiss her fingertips as she walked through the courtyard. She embraced Qing Shan and smiled at everyone warmly. Clearly the lady held no grudges.

Jia Yi recovered from her harrowing experience, and now Xianning included her wholeheartedly in his work. She wrote all of his dispatches and read over all of the messages sent to him. He was surprised one day when she told him why one of the battle plans had failed. Using checkers, she created a battle scene and demonstrated. His amazement was unbounded.

"How could you know battle tactics?"

Her ever-present pen quickly wrote her answer. *I have seen battles both in Europe and the*

Near West. It seems my life follows war. I saw why so many of the crusaders lost the battle. It was because their tactics were flawed against a more cunning adversary, and they refused to alter their formations to better withstand an assault.

She looked up at him. She thought her life followed war, and somehow that seemed tragic to have her feel this way. He kissed away her sad face and promised that whatever had happened in her travels, at least she had come to him. And that was the happiest thought he had ever had.

He found himself frequently holding council with her over his outgoing orders. She never ceased to astound him, her answers always showed wisdom and foresight.

They had a few, short, happy weeks together until Zhou Song came back into their lives.

Without evidence against him, Xianning decided to play ignorant of his enemy's intentions, with no sure proof it was deadly to accuse the emperor's favorite.

Zhou stayed to dinner, and though he said little, his wife said plenty. Zhou Daiyu talked relentlessly, and Jia Yi was a perfect hostess. Xianning adored every aspect of his wife now and mulled over the contrast of her darker skin compared to the marble white beauty of Lady Zhou. Jia Yi had embraced this culture she now lived in, and everything she did was a perfect complement to her gracious nature.

Lady Zhou saw this foreign girl as a threat to her reputation as a famed beauty. While her speech was littered with wit and humor, her eyes burned with fire. Lord Zhou watched the play with amusement and interjected comments, adding to the drama.

"I see she looks fine and healthy, I heard about her ordeal of course, but it mustn't have been too bad, judging by her appearance," Zhou remarked, his eyes flicking in Xianning's direction.

Xianning thought he would strangle his guests with the rage that swelled inside him. But he was too well trained for that. While his heart fumed, his impassive face showed no emotion.

"She is a brave woman, nothing seems to daunt her," he remarked, noticing the little smile that played in Jia Yi's face. She had heard his remark while pretending to mind her guest's conversation.

When at last they left, Jia Yi approached her husband. These days she didn't always need pen and paper to communicate. They understand many things between themselves.

"Yes, at last they're gone," he commented with a glance at her face. She smiled warmly and sat down on the chaise lounge with her fan cooling the insults she had received from Lady Zhou.

"That woman is insufferable." He agreed, taking the fan from her tiny hand and proceeding to fan her himself. She laughed her beautiful silent laugh.

"Perhaps, sometime, I will tell them just what I think of them," he said, laughing with her. "Lady Zhou's ears will ring for days if I do."

Behind his smiles, he was very worried though. He had pitted minds with Lord Zhou too long to doubt he was up to something, and Zhou had always been one step ahead of him before. It wasn't until that evening, he noticed one of his gloves had gone amiss. After unsuccessfully looking for he it, he lightly dismissed it as lost to Jia Yi. He gave the appearance of unconcerned, but he was sure that somehow Zhou or one of Zhou's attendants had taken it. It bothered him greatly as to why. Petty thievery was not part of Zhou's personality. Grimmer hobbies entertained his cruel mind, and the lost glove disturbed Xianning more than he cared to admit.

BEAUTY BEFORE WAR

Xianning had been home with his wife for nearly four months now, and they had been the happiest months of his life. For the first time, he dreaded a summons to return to battle. Yan Bin even commented about it one day. Xianning threw a piece of food at him, but he laughed too. Jia Yi was one of those rare people that was so pleasant to be around, even his warhorse was befriended by her.

Sometimes he found himself just watching her as she walked or even when she sat writing with her long lashes brushing her cheek. Could any man have had a more charming wife? He doubted it. Jia Yi was not stingy in her love toward him. It was the little things that said it, like when her fingertips brushed against his hand when serving food. It was so simple a gesture, and a little blush always crossed her face with it. He found himself living in those moments.

Occasionally, they went out and walked through the city. People always stared at her, some with annoyance because she was different, but many admired her. She had so long been an outcast that she never seemed to notice either way. She had met, by chance on one of their outings, a priest from the nearby temple. He had been buying goods in the market to create medicines. Her interest at his purchases had him invite the couple back to the temple to watch the process. She seemed to absorb information and Xianning watched as her quick mind understood medicines and treatment methods for various ailments. She had even helped to make some of the remedies, and when they left the priest said she was welcome to come study anytime she wished.

Xianning was always impressed at his wife's capabilities, and he had come to almost expect them, her brain could have been labeled as a genius. He thought wryly it was good the emperor only allowed boys to take the national exams for Jia Yi would have beat them all.

A few days later he received a message from Zhou. Hard lines creased his forehead as he read it. *The emperor has had restless dreams about the war. I told him everything that General Fu attended to was in good hands. I said well, don't you think?*

What was Zhou up to? He did not let his wife see the letter, but he knew that somehow she would sense a misgiving. The mastery he had over emotions was put into the strongest effort he had ever had.

But Jia Yi did notice his thoughts that night as they watched the teasing moonbeams playing on the floor. For several minutes, Jia Yi gazed steadily at her husband's face. He tried to ignore her questioning eyes at first. But her silent speech was loud tonight.

"It's nothing, my darling, perhaps I am just tired. Please do not give it another thought." Her gaze seemed to penetrate his mind as if she would read the worry there. He stood and walked over to her, gently taking her face in his hands.

"Please, it is nothing for you to worry over. Your mind should only be filled with happiness." He kissed her, but he felt she was not satisfied. Still, she was one of those wonderfully rare people who did not pry, and she let the matter drop. Her faith in her husband was so strong that she had no doubt he was capable of handling anything. Perhaps the only thing she had never shared with him was her deepest determination to die for him if necessary. But though she hid this level of passionate loyalty, he knew. He knew her too well maybe, and this was one problem he would hide with every ounce of his being. He would not let Zhou's threatening presence invade her peace if he could help it.

One evening a week later, as they headed home from a walk by the river, a little cat was seen crouching in a rain puddle. Jia Yi looked at her husband.

"Yes, you may bring it home."

He couldn't have said no if he wanted to, and he didn't want to. And a bothersome little gray cat moved in, wreaking havoc on the orderly household. He climbed walls, shredded garments, and reigned supreme master over the servants. But Jia Yi loved it, so Xianning was content to overlook the damages.

It was the cat that first found out. One afternoon after a heavy rain, with the bamboo trees dripping and the air heavy with the smell of earth, Jia Yi was sitting on a mat beside the pond feeding the koi fish. The cat went up to her and touched his nose to her stomach. The cat was not usually a particularly loving creature, but it weaved about, purring and seeming to smile up at Jia Yi's face.

Xianning noticed and paid close attention to his wife the next few days. She was dreamy and lost in thought often. The cat seemed very attentive and touched her more gently than before. He smiled as he told Qing Shan to call a physician.

The news was as he thought. Jia Yi was pregnant. They thought their hearts would burst with joy. Every servant doted over her, every guard was more reverent than before. The physician said six months from now a baby would be welcomed into the house. Jia Yi and Qing Shan began preparing baby clothes and would giggle between themselves, Jia Yi with her silent laugh that made Xianning laugh too.

He refused to let her do any more dispatch writing, but he still often discussed his orders with her.

After one such discussion, she sat, smiling and looking at him.

"I haven't thought of definite name yet," he said, answering her thought. Her eyes sparkled.

"But you have, I see."

She nodded and dipped the quill in ink. *Fu Liang Xui*.

He stood over her and read it, smiling and stroking her hair. "And if it's a boy?" he asked.

She wrote again, *That I'm still deciding*.

He laughed.

"Whatever we have, the name you choose will be perfect," he agreed.

She seemed sometimes to have an unearthly beauty about her, and tonight she certainly did. Xianning thought if the baby looked like her, it would be almost too much to bear to possess two such treasures. A flash of worry crossed her face for a moment, and she looked down.

"What's wrong?" he asked, leaning forward to look more closely at her eyes. She motioned to him, then to herself. "Ah, yes, you're worried what the future holds for a baby with mixed blood. Don't worry. Some people will be unforgiving of them, but as long as our children have us to love them, it will be all right. They will have a home and the world's most beautiful mother."

She pushed him away with a laugh, the worry gone. Her eyes said the children would have the world's finest father. He tapped her nose with a smile, and they enjoyed a quiet evening.

His joy was complete now, and his worries increased. Zhou had made no personal showing for weeks now. But the letter worried him just as much as if Zhou had spoken it in person. What was he up to?

And now Xianning protection duties were twice as anxious with the baby coming. Yan Bin was aware of the Zhou situation, and his humor-filled face was graver these days. Both felt a long shadow crawling toward the manor.

SCHEMES AND SHADOWS

A pale moon hung listlessly over the courtyard, ringed in by menacing clouds. Xianning stood staring at the sky, hands clasped behind his back. No wind stirred, no nightbird sang. There was a sinister brooding in the air as a storm maneuvered on the horizon. He heard distant thunder shatter the stillness, and a strong smell of rain flooded the night.

Walking back into the pavilion, he saw his wife kneeling with the cat in her lap. Xianning sometimes tried to approach her silently, just to see if he could. But her ears were too perfect, and she always turned about with a smile. His footstep was ingrained in her memory forever. She heard him tonight, his ability to walk silent as an assassin was still loud to her. She seemed worried behind her smile.

"It's just a storm," he said reassuringly. The cat crouched, frightened of the weather, hissing at the thunder crashes. Xianning pulled his wife carefully to her feet. "You really shouldn't get down on the floor. It's not safe with the baby on the way." She flashed a brilliant smile, the word *baby* always brought that same joy to her face. Snuggling the cat in her arms, she glanced outside as the rain began beating down on the earth.

Xianning stepped behind her and wrapped his arms about her waist. Both of them sensed something, but they didn't know what it was, and they didn't want to speak of it. Something felt wrong tonight.

It was when the storm was at its zenith that a snake slithered across the stone courtyard and into the pavilion. This was not like the harmless snake Xianning had released that day to test his wife; this reptile was a lethal Chinese cobra. Angry at being half-drowned, its lidless eyes roved about seeking revenge.

Xianning awoke, feeling something was wrong. Lightning lit the room for a second, but he did not see the creature that crept along the wall. He felt Jia Yi stir next to him, her eyes opened, and she stared at the ceiling. As if on impulse, they both sat up and looked at each other. The snake was now near the bed, but it still remained unseen.

Xianning pulled his knife from the wall above the bed and stood up slowly, looking about the dark interior. That's when the snake struck him. An intense fiery pain burned his foot, and he fell back against the bed. He was too much of a soldier to wonder what had happened; he knew it was a snake bite. His wife grabbed him and pulled him back up onto the bed, frightened and unsure of what had happened.

Xianning felt his foot slowly going numb, indescribable pain spread up his leg. His ankle was already swelling to twice its normal size.

Jia Yi tried to rise from the bed to run for help, but Xianning held her in a vise grip, afraid the snake would bite her too. Another flash of lightening lit the room, and she saw the reptile. Her eyes widened with horror as she realized what had happened. Yanking free from Xianning's grasp, she grabbed the knife from his shaking hand and proceeded to cut his foot, up his ankle as far as the purple poison line had worked in his skin. Blood began running to the floor. Xianning pried the knife away from her and the next lightning flash once again revealed the snake moving up the wall. The knife was thrown, and the snake was dead. Xianning collapsed back into the bed, and Jia Yi ran out to find Yan Bin.

Yan Bin awoke with a start to see his mistress soaked and sobbing in the doorway of his room. He immediately raced to his master and Jia Yi showed him the dead twitching snake. Yan bin ordered the servants to bring a physician. Xianning had lost a great deal of blood, which meant less poison was in his body—but a small amount of poison from a Chinese cobra could still be deadly. The physician came and said he saw little hope. Jia Yi left the manor at a dead run. When Yan Bin realized she had left, he chased after her, catching up at the temple where she had watched the priest make medicine. She clawed and banged on the gates, while Yan Bin shouted. The storm made it hard to be heard, but at last the priest came and opened the gate. He recognized his young prodigy, and Yan Bin quickly told him the situation.

The priest went inside and emerged moments later with a basket. They hurried back to the manor, and Jia Yi threw herself beside the bed, holding on to her husband's hand. Her tears and silent sobs broke everyone's heart. Xianning was pale, and his body shook with tremors, but he kept his eyes on his wife's grieving face. The priest assessed the wound, stopping the bleeding expertly, then drew Yan Bin aside.

"She thought quickly to save him. We must keep his wound clean now. I can rid his body of the remaining poison, but his fever must break within two days, or his body won't be able to process the medicine properly and he will die."

Yan Bin looked at the face of the man he served. "If his wife is by his side, he will live." The priest gave a half smile. "You seem confident."

Yan Bin turned and looked the priest in the eye. "That's because I'm sure."

Without further delay, the priest began making the medicine compound. Jia Yi helped but refused to stay away from Xianning's side for more than a few moments. Every three hours, the medicine was administered, and all the while Xianning's fever grew worse. The cobra's poison and the fever began to cause his brain to wander. He saw old memories coming back to life, and it caused him great agony. Jia Yi had a hard time keeping him calm while the nightmares raged. She never left his side for moment and Qing Shan feared for her lady's health and the baby. The household went about hushed and grieved as the master's fever worsened each hour. Jia Yi refused to let any servants in the room, with the exception of Yan Bin and Qing Shan. Xianning said many things in his fever that no one else needed to hear.

But Jia Yi realized so many things she had not known before. Xianning's parents had been killed when he was young. He had Qing Shan as his only family, and they wandered the countryside as vagabonds, until he was old enough to secure a job as a horse groom for an army camp. She pieced together that he had enlisted at a very early age, and his courage in battle had earned him the title of general straight from the emperor. But somehow a shadow of someone lurked throughout his life story. But either he did not know who or he would not say.

Jia Yi wrote a message and handed it to Yan Bin. *The snake was not a chance of fate. Find who did this.*

Yan Bin nodded. "Do you have a suspect, my lady?"

She wrote one word. *Zhou.* And her face said to find the proof.

PIECES AND PUZZLES

It was a still, foggy morning. Jia Yi had watched her husband's fever break only hours before, and the priest had said Xianning would certainly live now. Relived and exhausted, she had fallen asleep, kneeling beside the bed with her head on his hand.

Xianning's eyes opened as the first bird broke the morning stillness. He looked at his wife's pale sleeping face and smiled. Yan Bin entered at that moment and nearly shouted with joy, but Xianning motioned for him to be quiet. Yan Bin bowed respectfully and left to go shout his joy elsewhere.

Jia Yi stirred and opened her eyes. For a moment, she just stared, as if she didn't believe he was really awake.

"I'm here," Xianning said kindly.

Jia Yi fell against him sobbing. He had never seen her cry like this, and his heart ached to see her so distressed and happy at once.

"Jia Yi," he whispered, raising her face, "Jia Yi, you don't need to cry, all is well." And she smiled weakly, nearly smothering him with kisses and tears. Yan Bin reentered then with his usual calm demeanor restored. He smiled and waited until Jia Yi stood up holding onto

Xianning's hand, her face still streaked with tears but radiant with smiles.

Xianning motioned him forward. "Thank you for protecting my world while I was not able to do so myself." They smiled. As brothers, they faced too many battles and crises. They could not have said more if they wanted to.

Later the next day, Xianning was able to sit up for a meal and asked Yan Bin to join him. Jia Yi had finally been convinced to have a rest in her pavilion and was being lavishly tended to by the servants. Xianning waited until they were alone to ask the pressing questions.

"Do you have a report?"

Yan Bin nodded grimly. "I found a sack outside the gate smelling grossly of snake. And the sack also contained your missing glove."

Xianning was not surprised. "I assumed there is more to it than simply a misplaced glove," he remarked dryly.

Yan Bin continued, "I traced the snake to a toxin merchant who had a customer that wished to buy a cobra. This customer I could not find. His description was only a black cloak with his face obscured by the hood. The only noticeable thing was a ring of jade and pearl. So far, I have had no luck tracking that ring. I did trace the snake purchase back to a peddler from foreign places that could tame snakes with a flute. But I could not find him, only the last street he had lived in, and the instrument he has oddly left behind. I have no doubt your glove was used to train the snake to your scent. It was certainly an assassination attempt."

He pulled the mentioned flute out of his sleeve. "Peculiar instrument, no one knows quite how to play it. I asked some village musicians and one thought it came from the west." He handed it to Xianning, who looked it over carefully. It was a lead, but would it lead to answers?

Later in the afternoon, Jia Yi entered to serve tea and saw the flute. She looked surprised and wary. Her face asked, "Where did you get that?"

Xianning looked at her thoughtfully. "You have seen one before?"

She set the tea tray down and picked up the flute. She nodded and went for paper and ink. She sat beside the bed and wrote her answer quickly.

This flute is used by snake charmers in India. It's called a pungi. The snake charmers are a group called the Saperas and can train snakes to do many things from the sounds of the flute. They are quite hypnotized by the notes.

She looked it over and Xianning watched her face, a thought dawning on him. "Can you play it?"

She shook her head and wrote, *It takes many years to learn to play the pungi well. I wasn't in India long enough to master it.* She laughed a little as she penned, *My Arab father was not keen to have me play it either.* She put the flute and pen back down and began pouring tea.

"Would you know how to recognize a snake charmer?" Xianning looked at her gently, knowing she was the only one he could ask with any knowledge of such things, but he hated the fear it would bring.

She was thoughtful for a moment, then added to her paper, *Perhaps. Their eyes sometimes are rather strange, you know. They say it's from reading the minds of snakes.*

She handed him his tea then looked over at him sharply. She didn't need to write down what her mind was thinking as she looked at his face.

"Is that how the snake came here?"

Xianning didn't answer right away. Somehow, he felt that his antagonist was trying to make him suspect his wife of having a hand in this snake business. But he knew better. He watched her face looking wretched and tried to belay her fears. "Possibly it is connected, but it is nothing since the snake is dead."

She was definitely alarmed now. After a moment, she began writing again. *They spend months training their snakes. This snake is dead, the trainer will be looking for another snake to replace it.* She looked up. Her face was full a fear before writing again, "*You have to leave. If he sends another snake, the priest might not be able to save you again. And it's all my fault. Everywhere I go, my past follows me. It's come to curse you now.*" She dropped the pen and covered her face with her hands.

Xianning smiled a little and pulled her hands away so he could look her in the eyes. "Your past does not determine your future. You are well traveled. My enemies may be far traveled as well. It is not because you are cursed. Don't say such things about yourself."

Qing Shan entered then and finished helping serve dinner. Jia Yi hardly ate, though Qing Shan reprimanded her gently, "You must eat for the baby, my lady."

Jia Yi tried to eat, and Xianning worried about her. Everything had been too much for her lately. He determined to ease her mind quickly. That night he called his spies in and set them to work finding the snake charmer. He even called in his most elusive spy. His expertise was needed.

Yan Bin was the only one he really trusted to deal with finding the mysterious buyer of the snake. He rather felt that Jia Yi knew about everything, but she pretended not to. Yan Bin had told him how she was aware that Zhou was behind the attempt on his life. Xianning knew his wife was too clever to keep things hidden from her for long.

The next morning proved a true test for her mind and stamina. An unexpected group of ladies came for tea. And the head of the little gossip group was Lady Zhou herself.

MATCHING OF WITS

Lady Zhou arrived in grand ceremony unexpected and most unwelcome. The servants even seemed stilted on serving her and the other three ladies of power she had brought as her backup. She was here with no good intentions, and everyone knew it. Jia Yi went to meet them regally, and Xianning watched her go with fear. What was lady Zhou up to? He couldn't handle the apprehension and did something he was slightly ashamed of. He stood beneath a shadow behind the curtain on the outer porch. And he eavesdropped. Yan Bin stood with him while the servants pretended not to see as they served tea.

Jia Yi sat with her calmest demeanor, listening and nodding politely. Lady Zhou began her attack quickly. "My dear little friend"—Xianning grit his teeth in annoyance—"I have heard so many things about the Fu mansion. Of assassins and snakes and such things as made my blood run cold." *If her blood ran any colder, she would be dead* was the thought on Xianning's mind. "And of course, dear, you must put my mind at ease about all this. I was simply terrified for you, especially with"—here she pronounced her words very slowly—"a baby on the way." He could make out Jia Yi's face very faintly through the curtain, but she did not even flick an eyelid. She smiled and motioned for paper and pen. She wrote her most elegant style, and Qing Shan stood beside her to read it out.

"The lady Zhou flatters me with her concern. What fool would make such attempts on my husband's life? It is well known he is a master of kung fu and a great warrior in battle."

Lady Zhou smiled, and her eyes narrowed some. It was her first time to have Jia Yi state her mind before her. "But Lady Fu must be careful. The world is full of people who will take such risk, even against those that can clearly defend themselves. Enemies can be anywhere."

Jia Yi's pen responded. *As you have said, the world is full of such people. My lady must be nervous to travel outside of her gate.*

Lady Zhou could not help her face turning a paler shade on her marble face. She fluttered her fan and answered, "Of course, you are right, it can be so very hard to tell friend from foe. What does general Fu think of these terrible threats?"

Qing Shan read out, "The general does not consider such things as terrible threats, merely annoyances to be dealt with quickly. I am not concerned."

Xianning felt his heart rate raise with pride at Jia Yi's witty reply.

Lady Zhou fluttered her fan harder. "Truly you have a high opinion for his talents."

I have great trust in his abilities. And that has given me a high opinion of him indeed. But please, ladies, I feel so foolish to have the conversation be concerned with my life. Pray tell us, is there any news of yourselves? I hear the empress has chosen a bride for the crown prince.

Xianning smiled. *Oh, she was so clever.*

This last note turned the tide on Lady Zhou, for her companions pounced on a chance to talk and gossip about affairs and rumors of court, of which they had many dealings, professionally or otherwise.

Lady Zhou had lost her footing on the conversation and kept her face barely masked behind an irritated smile.

Yan Bin raised his eyebrows at the disgraceful way these ladies talked about other officials' wives. It really was enough to raise a blush at their shameless disregard of their court rivals.

When at last they rose to leave, Lady Zhou could not resist one more open attack. She smiled and commented to Jia Yi. "Lady Fu must be careful. Your travels in the past have had you brush shoulders with many unsavory characters, I'm sure. And as I said, it is hard to judge friend from foe. You can never tell who to trust."

Jia Yi wrote a last flourish. *Lady Zhou is most correct. One can brush shoulders with unsavory characters, even in one's own home. Do travel carefully. Foes are often the ones with smiles.*

Xianning and Yan Bin could hardly keep from laughing aloud and covered each other's mouths.

Jia Yi bowed to the guests while Lady Zhou bit her lip so hard it bled. The other three ladies seemed to rather like Jia Yi's clever company, and it had Lady Zhou looking like murder. They left rather abruptly at her command, and Jia Yi turned back to the porch. Xianning came out then and she laughed, her beautiful silent laugh, when she realized he was listening all the while. She sat, down shaking with her quiet mirth, and Xianning felt Yan Bin about to erupt in laughter as well. He dismissed himself quickly, and they could hear his smothered chuckles as he walked away.

Jia Yi looked archly at her husband. He smiled and replied, "I had to hear what she was up to, I apologize for my behavior."

She looked coy and smiled up at him.

"And yes, I also wanted to know what you would respond. My sin of spying is wrong, though it was worth it to hear you put the lady Zhou in her place."

Both laughed now, and the day ended on a happy note. But both knew that the Zhou's presence was always followed by a sinister intent. How would it happen though? Only time could tell. Would they ever be free of the threat from the Zhou's?

COMING TO THE SURFACE

Yan Bin had found information about the snake buyer. And he was troubled. His search had led him to ask questions and find answers that concerned his master's earlier life. There were many things Yan Bin had not previously known and was not sure if he should know. Fu Xianning was famous for keeping his personal life very private, and Yan Bin knew more about him than any other man. And yet today he found he really had known very little before.

The trail of the villain had led him to an old man in a nearby town, who was nearly deaf with age.

This man knew of someone who wore a ring of jade and pearl. He was very hesitant to speak on it, however, and Yan Bin was long in convincing him to share the information.

"Do not be afraid to tell me, I will protect you."

The man shook his head and smiled wryly. "At my age, I fear no man. The grave has long awaited me. I hesitate to speak because tragedy is a bitter thing to repeat."

Yan Bin sat down on the stoop and waited for the man to tell the story at his own pace. The story was very tragic and very bitter. A setting sun was fading on the horizon when the man concluded his tale. Yan Bin had paid the man a large sum for his time and was slow to make his way home. He traveled back through the evening before he reached his hometown. The darkness of night had long covered the village streets while he debated with himself. How could he tell this information to the general? Even if he just told the outline, it would be apparent that he knew many other things surrounding these facts.

He was walking with these thoughts when he became aware of eyes watching him. Instinct knew that the person was on the roof above him. With the precision he was trained for, he turned, grabbed the roof's edge, and swung up. The shadow moved, and Yan Bin struck. He was blocked and jumped when he heard the voice.

"Yan Bin, it's me."

"I'm sorry, master." He pulled away with a regretful bow. Xianning patted his shoulder. "You are well trained."

Xianning had met with one of his spies who had news and realized Yan Bin was very late returning. He had searched in his quiet way until he saw him in the street.

"Your face tells me you have news. My mind tells me you are hesitant to share it with me." The general was not one to hide information from, even if it was distressing to hear. They walked down to the river on the edge of the village, far away from any ears that might listen.

Yan Bin turned and faced his master, "Sir, I know who once owned the ring. And I suspect I know who now owns the ring."

Xianning seated himself in casual repose beside the river and locked his eyes on the swirling water. "Go on."

And Yan Bin told the whole story. Some things Xianning had already known and some things he had not. Xianning's surname was not Fu. That was his mother's family name. When he was three years old, his uncle and father had a fight. A very bad fight. Wounds had been given, and the feud was made worse because they had been very close brothers for years. They had fought because Xianning's father had been informed his brother had made collusions with a foreign leader to trade illegal goods across the border. Xianning's father as the elder brother had taken good care of the younger until this news came to him. He banished him from his house as a traitor to the country. But love for his brother kept him from exposing him to the authorities. His brother left and returned a year later with an edict from the emperor declaring the entire household treasonous and ordering their death. Xianning's nurse had hidden with little Xianning in the well. When it was quiet, she had crawled out to see them all slaughtered—the mother, father, servants and the servants' children. Even the horses had been killed. The nurse was Qing Shan's older sister, and she had fled the city with the child, living out on the frontier lines, close to the border and far from home. She stayed with her younger sister, under her lady's maiden name, terrified of being discovered but doing well by the child she was raising. Some of the past she told the boy as he grew, yet there were things she did not tell him. When Xianning was six, his nurse died, and Qing Shan became his caregiver. At age ten, he found work as a horse groom at a military outpost. He enlisted later and shortly afterward the first of the invasions began.

While Xianning was off winning battles, his uncle was home winning the emperor. He had produced the fake evidence that had killed his brother's family and was blissfully unaware that his nephew still lived. When he saw him presented at court to honor his deeds and elevate him to the position of general, the uncle was shocked and enraged to see his brother's line still lived. But he could not take him down openly. The army loved him too much and the Mongols feared him too much. The emperor would hesitate to take the life of this hero. The uncle's mind began manipulating; his tactics were perfectly precise. Every action was part of a well-laid scheme to bring about his nephew's demise.

The old man that had known these things of the long-forgotten past was a devoted guard for Xianning's father. He had been away that fatal day visiting his dying father. That is why he had survived, and years of silence was why he yet lived. Finding in his relentless search that the child was still alive, he had kept quiet to protect the young heir. He had silently kept his ear to the ground these many years and had long realized that the general living in the nearby village was his young master. The ring of jade and pearl had once been worn by Xianning's father, and his brother had taken it on the day of the slaughter.

The ring was given as a voucher to a man who knew how to kill and leave little trace. This man still eluded them, but his boss was now known. And Yan Bin finished with what Xianning was already realizing.

"Your family name is Zhou. And Zhou Song is your uncle."

Xianning did not speak for a moment. Finally, when at last he did, he only said, "You must pay that old guard well and see he lacks nothing for the rest of his life."

"Already done, sir. What should we do about Zhou?" Xianning looked over at Yan Bin, his most trusted servant and friend.

"How do you catch a tiger?" "With bait?"

Xianning smiled and nodded. "We simply need the right bait."

"But, sir, this tiger is quite deadly. How will you catch him and live to tell the tale?"

"We need to think with the same precision as Zhou. He is afraid of me. We must use that against him. We need a perfect plan. And I know someone who can help it come about."

MIND GAMES

It was early morning, and a stubborn fog still hung about, refusing to surrender the day to the sun. Xianning was practicing sword with Yan Bin in the courtyard while Jia Yi watched. As they blocked and thrust back and forth, Xianning was deep in thought. The sword was an extension of his arm, and he hardly considered what moves he made for his instinct was always at its paramount perfection. Yan Bin was practicing with a half-smile. He knew Xianning's mind was elsewhere, and yet he still could not defeat him in practice. Ten days ago, he had located the snake charmer and managed to steal a glimpse of a message written to the charmer. But it was written in Sanskrit. He had not been able to slip the note away much to his annoyance. Xianning had ordered him to only watch and not engage with this enemy. This morning he had seen the charmer watching the street eagerly. It could be assumed his employer was expected to rendezvous with him. He had left another man to watch the charmer's movements and had come back to report.

Xianning needed to think, which was why they were practicing swordsmanship, for he always thought his best when his hands were active. Finally, Xianning declared it was enough. They saluted each other and Jia Yi put down the cat she was cuddling to clap her admiration for their finesse. Xianning walked up to her, and she motioned toward the sword. He handed it to her and watched her flick it back and forth for a moment before handing it back. She would have been expert at any weapon she trained in as her mind absorbed knowledge and skill so quickly. But he would not train her while she was pregnant, even though she would often ask in her most winning way. And she asked again today.

"No, I won't. Someday, but not yet." She smiled and wrapped her hand in his as they walked into the pavilion. His mind whirled when he looked down at her, he would never have known what love could do to a person. He needed to tell her about his family history—and that his greatest enemy was also his uncle. He just could not understand how to begin the explanation. How to tell her his father's hesitation, perhaps even weakness, had given Zhou the upper hand? How to begin to explain the slaughter within his own family, of the cursed blood running through his veins?

Jia Yi felt his hesitation, though she didn't know the cause. She reached out, touching his face, her eyes full of understanding, giving him the will to speak. He took her other hand, the sound of the fountain soothing his apprehension. He sat down on the couch and pulled her into his lap. She smiled and waited. He stared off, not focusing on anything and told her. She was still the entire tale, and he finally glanced at her to see how she had received the news. Her eyes were so sad, he stopped talking to kiss her.

"What do you think of me know?" he whispered, dreading her answer.

She abruptly rose and crossed to his desk. He heard the pen rushing furiously across a page, and he walked over to see what she wished to tell him. In a strong bold hand, she had written, *You are not your father. And you are nothing like Zhou. You will defeat him, because you are a* good *man.*

He stared at the writing for a moment, then looked back at her face. She reached out and squeezed his hand hard.

"Yes, I know you will do anything to help me."

Her loyalty shone in her face, in the grip of her small hand. "We will win. We will."

She gave a small bounce on her toes, her eyes alight. Xianning nodded, taking comfort and courage from her faith in him. Today he had to put all of his energy to action, for today the tiger hunt must begin. And there was no sharper mind than Jia Yi to help him begin it.

"I need you to write a letter in Sanskrit for me," he said as they walked through the cool interior of the house. She was surprised but nodded without hesitation.

"Yes, it's an odd request, but I need to enact a plan to find the snake charmer's accomplice." This answer she found quite satisfactory and once again found pen and paper, then sat awaiting his instructions.

She was eager to help him, and she was afraid for her husband so long as the snake charmer was on the loose. And she was determined to not let Zhou beat him. Xianning knew that being involved would help her fears, and no one else could have the talent to write in Sanskrit. He smiled a little as he dictated.

"Write this: found a new snake, meet me at the top of the temple tonight at dusk, and I will deliver it to you. Do not fail to show or your ancestors will be speaking with you in person. And sign it 'a ring of pearl and jade.'" She finished writing and handed the letter to him.

"Yan Bin has seen him reading from a Hindu prayer book, as well as seen a past message he has received from his employer, so I know he is literate. I'm taking a bit of a risk to assume that he will not be surprised to receive this type of instruction. I am also positive he does not know his employer's name, but the mention of the ring will speak for itself. I have a street vendor willing to deliver for money and no questions." He glanced thoughtfully at the foreign writing. "You're remarkable," he stated, and Jia Yi blushed with pleasure. Her face showed she knew that her husband would be meeting with this villain, but so long as the snake charmer was devoid of snakes, she was not concerned. She had too much faith in Xianning's skill to worry about him in that regard. Xianning, though, was worried. This plan could not deviate, or Zhou would smell him coming and then have his evidence to take to the emperor. And then Jia Yi's life would be at risk, which was his only concern, for he hardly thought of himself in terms of danger. But Xianning was one of those people who, when concerned, become more determined to succeed.

The letter was delivered, and Yan Bin had returned to his post of watching the charmer. Xianning tended to his work as usual, and no one could have guessed the dangerous evening he had planned.

Jia Yi hardly left his side all day, and when evening approached, she grew very anxious. Xianning noticed and stopped working to take her for a walk in the garden. Her hand grasped tightly to his arm, and her face said so many things. Xianning was uncharacteristically amusing this evening and soon had her smiling and laughing—worry was still there, but for a moment she could ignore it.

When it was time to leave, Xianning brought out a cape he had ordered to be made, the color and material matching the description of the one worn by the owner of the infamous ring. This plan he had been formulating since he had first learned of this individual, to mimic his appearance and appear before the snake man. His last part of costume was a replica, quickly made by a jeweler that loved money more than gossip. He slipped a ring of pearl and jade onto his finger. It was made to closely resemble the old guard's description of the infamous piece. Finally, tonight all was ready to put it into action.

Jia Yi had stood for a moment with him, waiting for the time to leave. He looked at her blue eyes, full of fear for him, and stooped to kiss her before swinging up to the rooftop and vanishing into the oncoming night shadows. He refused to look back, for her face would be begging to come and help. And that was one thing he would not allow.

When the last vestige of sunset was gone, he stood on the roof of the temple, watching the lanterns light up across the world at his feet. The snake charmer was a bit late coming. He heard a sound and pulled his hood lower over his face. A small man, with a back bent from years of hovering over snake baskets, was dragging himself up the last step to the top terrace. Xianning dropped down to the terrace and stood well within shadow to watch the approach. The charmer saw him, and his eyes narrowed.

Xianning saw what Jia Yi meant by the eyes of a snake charmer being strange. They were eerie and dilated, and it seemed as if he could see well in the darkness.

The charmer bowed and waited for a sign. Xianning guessed it and held up his hand adorned with the false ring. Feeling secure now, the charmer spoke in a soft musical voice.

"I thought my lord said he had no further need of my services. Aren't you going to pay me as promised, so I may return to my homeland? You brought me here from my travels abroad, and in my journeys, I have been many years away. Why do you suddenly require another snake to be trained?" His Chinese pronunciation was very good. Xianning reached under his cloak and pulled a leather sack meant to be containing the snake. The charmer hesitated. "This man must be very much hated for my lord to be so determined. My last snake, as you will recall, did not fail. But this enemy has a clever wife, I hear, and removed the toxin so quickly that he yet lives. I do not think a second snake will achieve even half as far. Now they are looking for me and my methods. I wish to return home. But…" He held his hand up and a greedy look came into his eyes. "For a modest fee, my lord, I can show you another way. And if I show you, then you must pay me tonight and release me on my way." Xianning nodded and jingled his purse to show he had gold.

"My lord is certainly determined to destroy his enemy. I know you have never once spoken in any of our meetings. Only by notes or messengers do I know your thoughts. But for this, my lord must repeat after me so I will know you understand it well. It must be carried out precisely or it won't work."

Xianning nodded, and the lethal plan was explained and repeated in all its gruesome detail.

BENEATH A PALE MOON

Jia Yi stood long into the night, watching the moon march across the ebony sky. Sunrise was painting the eastern edge of the world when at last Xianning appeared. His face was stern and his jaw set. He stopped and looked at Jia Yi for a moment. Her look of relief hurt him. The snake charmer had set his heart in turmoil. He knew would have to send her away to keep her safe. Zhou's plan now was to destroy Xianning's greatest treasure. He knew this would kill him without having to soil his hands with the blood of China's youngest general.

She wanted to know what had happened, had he discovered anything, and what was his next plan. But mostly her thoughts just said she was so glad he was back. He couldn't answer her questions. Instead, he stepped up and wrapped her in a protective hug. He felt the baby kick in her stomach, and he knew his heart would break if he never got to meet Jia Yi's baby. He had to protect them both at all costs, even if they had to flee the country.

Yan Bin stood at a respectful distance watching his master, and he knew that Xianning was in a bitter turmoil. And he hated Zhou for his master's sake. The charmer had revealed a ghastly murder plan for Jia Yi, but he had told the wrong bearer the ring, so the assassin was not plotting currently with this method. And now the charmer was too dead himself to assist in any further murders. But it was only a matter of time. They had to catch the shadow before he came again. The charmer knew of a poison that killed slowly, cruelly, and was irreversible—a poison that had come from India. Jia Yi would likely know of it. If he mentioned it, she would fear it was meant for her husband; she could not understand that Zhou's hate for his nephew had led him to hate his nephew's wife this much. He didn't answer her silent questions, he couldn't speak. He gripped her a little tighter and kissed her silken hair. Then he grabbed her hand and led her inside. Until he had her safely hid away, he would not let her out of his sight. Yan Bin and Qing Shan were the only ones who would know the plans. He feared that someone else might let it slip, and the enemy spies would hear of it. He would have died a thousand times rather than see harm come to his wife. He understood one thing very clearly: he was the son of a long blood feud between his father and his uncle. But that did not mean he must follow the same mistakes.

His father had been too lenient, and his uncle had been a murderer. Xianning would deal with his family, but he would not be like either of them. He was the descendant of them, but he would not be the protege of a tragic family past.

He held Jia Yi's hand almost all day as he worked, only releasing her so she could eat. She watched him, and he knew that she had guessed it; he was sending her away. He could sense she was displeased, but she doted on him like never before. Perhaps she was trying to convince him he couldn't live without her. He smiled inside, for that was certainly true, but he loved her too much to risk her just to keep his own heart from breaking from her absence.

As afternoon approached a royal courier came. The entire household came out and went to their knees in the presence of the emperor's words. Xianning felt his heart grow cold. This was exactly how his family had been that fatal day so long ago. The courier unrolled the scroll and read the words.

"This household is suspected of housing a traitor to my esteemed, supreme self. Until the traitor is found, this household will remain within these walls and be investigated."

Xianning accepted the scroll and said his dutiful words of acceptance to the decrees. Only those who knew him well saw the fire in his eyes. If Zhou had dared to appear at the moment, his life would not have been worth the cost of an epitaph. Everyone to the lowest servant knew that Lord Zhou had arranged this house arrest. Royal guards surrounded the outside of the house. It was not a good day to work in the Fu household.

Xianning realized that Zhou had discovered his impersonation of the assassin. He had set the stage now, knowing Xianning would try to hide Jia Yi safely away, and he had trapped them by the emperor's decree. Chains would not have held them in such a stranglehold.

The courier left, and everyone scuttled away fearful, and yet there was a certain loyal anger with the household. That the emperor should think such a great general would house a traitor was insulting to the pride they had in their master.

Xianning sat down at his desk in silence. But his face was a battlefield. How did Zhou receive his information so quickly? Yet no, he had received it before even Xianning had impersonated the assassin.

The emperor's decree should have taken several days to travel to them from the capital. Yet only yesterday had the impersonation plan been enacted. Zhou had plotted even this. He had studied his opponent so long he knew his very thoughts. Xianning was enraged at himself for being so obvious. And yet, as a general, this tactic had the second half yet to be played. The counterattack. The hammer had struck, but the gong was still to ring.

A grim smile played on his mouth. And the idea was forming—but with an edge Zhou could not foresee. He judged his nephew as he had judged his brother. But Xianning had not earned the title "China's youngest general" for nothing. He would not wait for the next move: he would strike first.

Jia Yi stood beside him and waited. Yan Bin stayed out of sight but within call. The line so long drawn between these two men was turning red. So often the upper hand had swayed between the two, yet now it was past the time of mind games. Now it was going to draw blood. Someone was going to die soon.

SETTING MOONS AND RISING SUNS

The sun rose on a new day of uncertainty. The house arrest had been enforced for forty-eight hours so far, and the dwelling had been ransacked and ruthlessly searched for the supposed traitor that was said to be housed by the Fu family. Xianning had wisely disposed of the duplicate jade ring, dropping it into the koi pond as the guards first entered the manor. The search had been concluded with nothing of suspicion unearthed, and now the guards patrolled the exits to keep the inhabitants inside until new orders arrived from the emperor.

Xianning spent the day in silence while guards marched around the walls outside. They had at last given his household some privacy. His mind had worked a plan, but it still could backfire, and it would leave Jia Yi alone, which scared him and was the only reason he still sat, hesitating within himself.

Finally, Jia Yi touched his hand, pulling him from his reverie. He looked up into her eyes, so full of love and trust. He looked at her stomach and thought of the baby inside waiting to meet its mother.

He saw Yan Bin watching them, his hand restless with no sword hilt to rest it on. The weapons had been taken away by the emperor's orders. Xianning smiled a little to himself, for he well knew Yan Bin still had at least three weapons hidden on his person. Too many battles and captures and escapes were shared between for Xianning to doubt this summarization. He stood up and took Jia Yi's hand and motioned Yan Bin to come forward.

"Have you noticed the change of the wind? A storm is coming today." Yan Bin nodded. "The first storm of autumn is always bad."

Xianning looked at Jia Yi then said, "I think I will provide the lightning, and we shall see if Zhou brings the thunder."

He whispered his plans to them with the cat as the third confidant. The cat purred and watched with big eyes, unknowing he was another piece to the scheme.

"Jia Yi, do you think the cat still remembers the skill you taught him?" She gave him a look that said *No doubt*.

"Send him to it tonight, before the storm breaks. Yan Bin, you will then proceed with your part of the plan, let your hawk then play his hand. Let us hope it is the beginnings of our favor changing."

So that night, with no moon and distant thunder, a cat silently slipped through a hole in the wall and made its way like a shadow to the temple. The cat had been taught by Jia Yi to go meet the priest with a pouch containing a note to send medicines should Jia Yi be sick during her pregnancy. The priest would then mix the herbs and fill the pouch for the little courier who would return home. But tonight the note in the pouch held something else: directions for the priest to send a messenger to the old guard that had long ago been part of the Xianning's family. And directions were to be given to the faithful guard on how to contact one of Xianning's spies. This message would be delivered to the spy.

An ill wind blows, only Zhou knows.

The spy would know this was Xianning's last stand message. All of his spies knew it. It meant the master's back was to a wall, and he was giving one more desperate fight. All of the spies would be mustered to await Xianning's next order. Yan Bin's hawk was trained to a unique whistle, and the spies would come to his call. The hawk would be at the rendezvous point until Xianning arrived to send him back to Yan Bin.

The cat returned soon, bristling against his fear of thunderstorms, anxious to reach the safety of Jia Yi's arms. The pouch was opened with instructions and the medicine inside. The monk had read their message and was willing to risk his life to help the couple. Jia Yi stirred the noxious powder into a cup of tea and, pausing to give Xianning a loving look, drank it.

The sedative soon worked. Jia Yi turned pale and fell into what appeared to be a fevered sleep. It was harmless and would cause no true discomfort to mother or baby. The medicine was a trick used to improvise a fever and had been used as subterfuge in the past. Xianning only hoped the guards outside his home would fall for the ruse. Soon he sent a servant to the head guard, begging permission to call a physician as his wife was ill. The head guard, Guang, was of the emperor's elite and was not easily fooled. He came to see himself and stood beside Jia Yi's bed, staring down at her sweating face. His frown was dark, and Yan Bin looked uneasily at his general, prepared to be extreme should the need arise.

Xianning remained unmoved, staring at a wall, hands clasp behind his back.

"Is she carrying your heir?" Guang asked, his fingers draped around his sword hilt. "Yes," Xianning replied calm, quiet.

"I am under strict orders to let no one in this house die until the emperor gives the command." He paused. "Or of course sees fit to spare you." He said it carelessly, and Xianning knew the former decree was far more likely.

"Send for a physician." The guard ordered, and Yan Bin bowed and left the room. They knew the monk would come when asked. He had already proved his loyalty to Fu Jia Yi by sending the medicine. The monk did come. The guard stood by suspiciously while the monk checked her pulse and felt her forehead. He shook his head ruefully, then with great decorum he turned.

"I can do nothing for her. She must sleep, and we will know in the morning."

The guard looked shocked. "No, monk, you cure her or else!" His voice was powerful.

"Perhaps a quieter tone would befit a sick room better," the monk said, unmoved by the angry voice.

The guard stepped close and spoke searingly. "She will not die on my watch, monk. Do not think your vocation will spare you from my sword should she die."

The monk did not even blink. "As I said, I can do nothing for her. I can order cool water to bathe her hands in hopes to bring the fever down. But I hardly need to stand over her. Her life is out of my hands." The monk had not spoken any lies, but he played the visage well.

"Be gone then, but I will draw your blood if she dies." Guang turned on a heel and left the room. Jia Yi was truly asleep and was uncomfortably hot—but not near death in any way. Soon a monk was leaving the house, the storm now breaking overhead. He bowed respectfully to the guards, who hardly gave him enough regard for a flea. Stepping down the road where rain now ran into rivers was Fu Xianning in disguise, heading to rendezvous with his league of spies. Inside the house, beside a pale Jia Yi, stood the monk, dressed as the lord of the Fu household. They had very little time before they were found out.

IS BLOOD THICKER THAN WATER?

Xianning had his meeting the next evening. Spies raced away to play their part. Birds flew carrying messages to every ally Xianning had while the hawk returned to Yan Bin.

Soon Xianning was thundering down the road toward the capital on the fastest horse that could be procured. Fresh horses would be waiting along the way. It was a seven-day journey to the capital city.

Xianning made it in five. Now dressed as a palace guard (having several people as allies in government positions definitely had its benefits), he made his way with arrogant bravado through the busy streets.

For three full days, he kept his ear to the ground and waited. His friends had been documenting every illegal trade and had finally pinned a lead to Zhou. They still had no proof that Zhou was associated with the Mongols, but at least they had something. Xianning's plan was laid like pieces to a game. All must go exactly as set. Tomorrow it would begin. It was time to expose Zhou to the emperor.

The morning sky shone blood-red across the city. As many as he could count on would be in court today before the emperor. It was a decree day, which meant Xianning's sentence would likely be decided before the sun had set.

His friends were not the most powerful, but they were many. His integrity and success in battle had won him more than people's admiration. He refused to dwell on Jia Yi, he could not think of her alone, afraid in her silence, wondering if he was succeeding. He had determined, since Zhou had played his hand, today would be the end of it.

He came into the palace walls with little concern. A few friends among the guard aided him, but they could do nothing more. He had to carry on the masquerade alone. His armor disguise was high enough to give clearance but not so high as to attract attention. Marching in with a slew of other guards, he took his place along the wall, standing in perfect form. He knew this role well. In his visits to the emperor, he had paid close attention to guards and security. It was how his mind worked, and today he was grateful to possess a military background.

As decrees were read, arguments made, bows, grovels, praises, and shouts arose as some people were dragged away to be forever silenced by the emperor's guards. The emperor was in a purging mood and had ransacked through his advisors. Traitors, spies, usurpers—whatever it pleased him to call them and give credence to his murderous rampage. So far none of Xianning's associates had met with the emperor's wrath.

Xianning remained in true guard form, motionless and emotionless. His eyes roamed cautiously until he saw Zhou standing near the stairs that led up to the throne. His smugness left no doubt in Xianning's mind that Zhou was behind the killing spree within the court. How did Zhou retain his hold over the emperor, how did he always stay court favorite? Xianning could have ground his teeth in rage as he watched Zhou's evident pleasure at the sentencing. Xianning remained stoic; however, he could not help these people.

He felt movement to his right and glanced out of the corner of his eye. The guard that stood a few feet away had moved his fingertips. Guards did not move; they were to be as statues, nonexistent unless the emperor was in danger or gave them orders.

Then the guard flexed his hand, so slight a movement, but so deliberate, the veins in his hand bulging. Xianning felt his entire body tense. The ring. The guard was wearing Zhou's ring. A ring of jade and pearl. The assassin.

Xianning's eyes raised to the man's face, still keeping his posture facing forward. The guard was staring at Xianning out of the corner of his eye. Slowly, deliberately, he smiled wickedly. His hand flexed again. The assassin had planned this moment so well that for the first time in his life, Xianning felt frozen with shock.

For a long moment, they remained still, no one in the room seeing this uncanny drama along the wall. Xianning was armed with numerous hidden weapons, and he well knew the assassin was as well. This man of mystery was his only aim in life to do Zhou's bidding, like a raging hound who only followed commands from one voice.

Suddenly, Xianning heard a name announced and glanced back to the throne. "What does his most esteemed emperor deem to sentence for the Fu family?"

Zhou had spoken. The emperor looked out at the crowd, and a heavy silence hovered. Xianning saw a flick of black above. Yan Bin's hawk had flown in and landed in the rafters. How the hawk had entered he didn't care, but the hawk was not supposed to be here. He was supposed to be miles away with his master watching over Jia Yi. Something had gone awry. The assassin saw the hawk as well and smiled again.

The scroll bearing the Fu family's fate was unrolled. The scribe cleared his throat to read. Everything seemed to be in slow motion as Zhou turned and raising his hand pointed at Xianning.

"He is here!"

The crowd surged toward him, the assassin vanished into the crowd, and Xianning suddenly knew what the plan was. Zhou had always known Xianning's plans, had always been one step ahead and had used his predictions for this moment. It was all a plot to assassinate the emperor, laying the blame on the Fu family, ending them once and for all. Zhou would then destroy the king's sons, who were admittedly fools. Zhou planned to rule all of the land; Zhou would be emperor.

The guards charged him, and Xianning fought them as if every one of them was Zhou himself. Above in the rafters, the hawk let out a shriek, and Xianning saw the assassin poised in a shadow, a blow dart in his mouth—another weapon from India. In a moment, Xianning was in the rafters, the hawk responding to his whistle command, charging into the assassin's face. The dart hit the bird, and the assassin's left eye was missing. He turned his ghastly wounded face to Xianning, his hand holding a curved dagger. Below there were shouts of confusion as people shouted pleas to the emperor over the commands of Zhou. The Fu family still had friends.

The assassin leaped, and the two began a duel, balancing among the decorative rafters. Below the room became eerily silent. Xianning did not have time to wonder why. The assassin, even with only one eye, was lethal in every move. Xianning was cut, once, twice, thrice. The curved blade was more accurate than the blow dart.

Xianning backflipped, grabbing on to an elaborate silk curtain and swinging over behind his opponent. The assassin was already prepared, and the two locked for a moment, frozen, staring into each other's faces. There was a hissing sound, and a snake crawled out of the assassin's sleeve. Lurching toward Xianning's hand, he rapidly pulled back as the assassin kicked out. He pivoted, missed the rafter, and fell.

He twisted in the air, just barely landing on his feet as the assassin landed in front of him, the snake now wrapped about his neck.

A sudden whistle, low and eerily haunting, flooded the silence. The assassin's remaining eye opened wide; the snake responded to the command and bit its own master. The man began shaking violently, finally dropping to his knees, his eye glazing over as blood came from his mouth and nose. The snake slid away from the dying man, and Xianning promptly beheaded the reptile.

Slowly, he looked up at the crowd, whose eyes were riveted to the throne. He followed their gaze and saw Zhou standing near the emperor, and beside the emperor stood Ilchidey. He was holding a familiar pipe. So Ilchidey had learned the art of snake charming as well. Xianning ground his teeth with rage at seeing the man who tried to destroy his wife a few months before—the only man he hated as much as he hated Zhou.

The poisoned hawk lay dead near the emperor's feet. Yan Bin would grieve the loss of his companion. A blade was poised at the emperor's neck. The guards all stood, weapons drawn to defend their ruler, but they would only achieve in killing his murderer. Xianning was too late. They were all too late. Zhou had won.

THE STARS ALIGN

Zhou made a mock show of horror at Ilchidey's position. The blade hovered off the emperor's neck, and yet he did not move in for the kill.

"Today I kill your leader, and you will have no time to mourn before we are at your door. The Mongols are coming, the Mongols are here!" Ilchidey's voice rang throughout the rooms. The fool, did he not know Zhou would dispose of him once he had thoroughly used him to achieve his end? Muqali could afford to lose this hothead captain. He had others that followed orders better and possessed fewer vices.

Muqali and Zhou had made an alliance that would take all of Asia to its knees. And no one could stop them now.

There was a hissing sound overhead, and Xianning lurched as an arrow sunk into Ilchidey's neck, sticking out the other side. Ilchidey's body shuddered and fell into the emperor, who kicked his lifeless form away and leapt to his feet. The room erupted in shouts and confusion.

"Seize the archer!" the emperor shouted, not waiting for silence to reign.

Looking back, Xianning saw the old man, the former guard of his family's house standing, bow in hand, quiver empty. He had only brought one arrow. The guards dragged him to the steps below the throne. The old man's face was complacent, calm amid the fury around him.

Xianning reached down and snatched the ring of jade and pearl from the assassin's finger. He felt the guards grab him as well, and he was pulled toward the throne. Zhou had adopted a neutral expression. His plan had partly failed, but he could still destroy Xianning. That at least was something, and a sneer played on his pale lips. The emperor was still standing, his eyes on fire with rage, his hand shaking in a fist.

"Explain yourself, Fu Xianning!" he thundered, pointing at Xianning's face. Xianning was forced to kneel, and he answered, surprised at how calm his own voice was.

"I have come to foil a dastardly plan to destroy my family and your most gracious self." He was now playing the politician. It was the only hand he had left to play.

"You do better than that, I have heard you praised as the tiger of the battlefield, but tigers are rogues that cannot be trusted."

"Vicious as a tiger can be, it never eats its own cubs. You are betrayed, sire. The tiger is not to be feared but the ant already in your ear."

"You accuse my advisors?" was the emperor's thundering accusation. "Only one, your majesty. It only takes one ant to destroy a whole dam."

"Stop quoting philosophers to me, a traitor your family has been and always will be!" "Then you should meet my uncle, sire." And Xianning calmly pointed at Zhou.

"What is this?" the emperor said, anger mixed with doubt in his face.

"You cannot believe the words of a liar, for each truth is sprinkled with ten falsehoods," Zhou replied shrewdly. But there was just the barest show of disquiet on his face. It seemed he did not realize that Xianning knew of their family ties.

"Enough wise quotes, I want direct answers!" The emperor was in a dangerous fury. A quiet voice cut through the silence. "May I speak, oh esteemed sovereign?"

The monk was here. Xianning could not understand how, but here he was. He very calmly and deliberately walked to the stairs and bowed. The men of religion rarely were denied a chance to speak as it was thought to be unlucky, and Xianning smiled inside at the monk's clever approach. The emperor nodded, and the monk continued. "If your most wise self thinks for a moment, you will see the truth. Who has trade in foreign parts with diplomats? Who has easiest access to your most sovereign person? Who has brought all of the accusations to the Fu family? Why was the Fu family killed those years ago, by whose word were they condemned?"

The emperor stared long and hard at Zhou, who still masterfully kept his mask of composure. "If I may, sire?" The old guard's voice was thin but undaunted.

"Speak," the emperor said without turning away from Zhou.

"I was there that day. I saw Zhou leaving town and returned to see my master's household slaughtered. Zhou's brother was Zhou Long. He is the dragon child of the family, who had his own brother killed and family burned. He has hidden his scales in a cloak of riches, but beneath it all he is still a dragon."

There was a silence, and for the first time, Zhou seemed troubled. He did not know until this moment that any servants survived from that day, let alone an eyewitness.

"The family of Fu Xianning—actually Zhou Xianning—has been called traitors, but the only traitor is the man who stands as your most trusted. He is the thief, the traitor, the murderer of his own kind."

There was a long silence in the room.

"Everyone not involved. Leave now." The emperor's voice was low. Cold. Commanding. Like sentencing one to death. The room emptied, save for Zhou, Xianning, the old guard, the monk, and a small group of palace police.

Xianning shrugged the palace guards' hands away and stood. "I am here to avenge the bane of my family. And see that my uncle receives his just dues for the sake of his dead brother, my father."

"I will kill you both!" the emperor shouted. But Zhou smirked and raised his hand, a ring of pearl and jade on it. Xianning reeled. How could there be two such rings? Was it a duplicate? Even the one he had created lacked the finesse of this original ring. But no, the one he held and the one in Zhou's hands were too perfect to be a fake.

"I expected you would do so, Zhou." The emperor's voice seemed suddenly deflated. Ah, so the ring was the power that Zhou possessed over the emperor.

Zhou spoke, "His majesty knows that you gave me this ring with a spoken vow and I may ask any favor and be not denied. And I yet possess the written decree you gave with it."

The emperor nodded, his shoulders sagging, and sat back down.

"I ask to spare my life and let me prove my unfailing loyalty to your royal self." Zhou bowed a bit mockingly.

"Two rings made, and two rings given to you and your brother. When you saved my life from assassins after I first became emperor." The emperor spoke with a tone of bitterness.

Zhou smiled coolly. "A worthy thing it was to save you."

"I have often thought it odd that your brother did not present his at his death warrant. His refusal to demand his right shows he was guilty."

"As I have said many times." Zhou's voice sounded like a snake hissing.

The emperor turned his full fury to Xianning now. But Xianning's mind was quick. He stood to his full height and raised his own ring of jade and pearl—a ring that he hoped would be honored.

"Grant me my request for the sake of the promise made to my father." His voice carried in the massive hall.

"How did that come into your possession? It should have been burned with your father's body." The emperor's voice was dry, as if Xianning's own father had stood as a ghost before him.

"My uncle preserved it, after the murder of my father, and it has since served his own evil ends." Now the royal rage was truly unleashed.

The emperor's voice exploded. *"How dare you use my own gracious decree to manipulate! Is that why Zhou Long did not present it, to save his life and his family? You had robbed him of my gift!"*

Zhou dropped to his knees, his face white. "I was saving it to return to you." His voice lacked all of the usual vice.

"It was in the assassin's possession," the monk said it quietly, but all heard. The emperor's eyes bulged with his rage. He stepped toward Zhou, then stopped. He looked back at Xianning.

"I will slay all of the accused Zhou family and rid my court of the name. But I suppose you intend to beg your life be spared, should I choose to honor the promise to your father."

Xianning smiled grimly. "No, I request the right to fight my uncle to the death. If he dies, my household is innocent and shall be spared."

The emperor stopped, for a moment shocked, but he saw this as a way out without breaking his word to Zhou. A grim and not-very-pleasant smile played on his face.

"So be it. Let the ancestors decide."

Zhou stood slowly and faced Xianning. The malicious look had returned to his oily face.

Both were given swords. The monk stood beside Xianning and whispered, "Do not let his apathetic movements fool you. He is deadly with a sword."

The swordsmen stepped toward each other, and the onlookers formed a ring around them.

I have so yearned to bring justice to my family. At last, it is here, Xianning thought grimly.

Zhou poised his blade. "Let us end this, nephew."

WHERE ONCE WE MET

There was a still moment. Then blades met. The air rang louder with each clash. Both opponents held back just a little, waiting to test the other, waiting to surprise the other with unknown skills. And yet even so the sounds of impending death ripped through the palace. The observers stood tense, silent, the emperor leaned forward, eyes trained intently on the moment. Everyone knew that these two men were highly skilled, but seeing them engaged in deadly battle, it was evident that perhaps the two greatest swordsmen in the land were dueling.

Zhou drew first blood, his eyes gleaming with malice. Xianning smiled a little, the blood running down his free arm, dripping from his fingertips to the polished floor. The ear-shattering sounds of clashing continued. It was a long battle. It was long in coming and deserved its fair time. Both were sweating and now both were bleeding.

Xianning had allowed himself to wound first. It was a tactic he had used on the battlefield before. To let an equal foe think himself superior was a great advantage. He had seen shock, rage, fear, and even crazed laughs when he fully unleashed onto his unsuspecting opponent.

"Hold back, until you can take all," his sword master had said those words so often. It was well-known that Zhou had trained many years previously with the same sword master. It showed.

They continued the dance of blades, then came up with the same move into a deadly lock. Their eyes were both strained on the other. Xianning's face, inches from his uncle's murderous gaze, could not help the words from escaping. "Why, uncle?" He wished he hadn't spoken, but all these years, these mind games…for what?

Zhou's mouth dipped into something like a snarl. "Because I hated your father, so I hate you," he whispered. They broke apart, slicing the air.

Then came the unplanned slip. Xianning blocked and stepped forward, only to slip in a puddle of blood. He slid, his balance precarious, his wounds seeming to handicap his recovery. Zhou gave a roar and surged forward to thrust the winning stab.

Zhou had either never learned or perhaps never listened to the sword master's warning against eagerness. *Do not be too eager, your enemy may be toying with your impatience.*

Zhou's blade raced to Xianning's heart. Xianning *was* toying. His wounds did not bother him as he pretended; he had fought with more wounds and less blood many times in battle. He leaned sideways, the back of his free hand flashing out, deflecting the metal and losing all skin on it while his own sword slid into Zhou's neck. His uncle's eyes grew large. He dropped his weapon and grabbed Xianning's shoulder. For a moment they stood, faces only inches apart. Then Zhou gave a slithering grin. His voice came out in a grating whisper. "And yet in the end, I've still won."

He dropped to his knees, gasped, and crashed down. The greatest enemy of the kingdom lay dead at Xianning's feet. And Xianning was at last avenged. The room was deadly silent. But he felt no victory. Panic gripped his throat. Zhou had always been two steps ahead. What had he done to insure he had won?

Jia Yi.

What had Zhou done now? His wife, he had to get to her. He turned and bowed low to the emperor. "My lord, greatest hero and protector, please speak whatever punishment you deem I deserve, but grant me a last favor."

The emperor slowly sat down, his posture resuming a kingly demeanor. There was a silence. Xianning was staring very hard at the gilded floor, sweat dripping from his face and blood dripping from his wounds.

"What favor would you ask? Your family line is ended, your enemies are laid to rest, the army thinks you're a hero. You're perhaps too lucky. What favor do you deem necessary to beg for?"

Xianning's voice was firm, low, but no one could mistake the heart in it.

"That I see my wife and have her future safely seen to before I meet my end." "Is she such a great woman? She is a barbarian slave, is she not?"

"She is my sun, my stars, and my moon." The quiet room felt a little queer, for power or money would have been the greatest thing to them. And yet here stood a hero of China saying his greatest treasure was his wife. "Then you must send me gift to thank me for giving her to you."

Xianning looked up, but the emperor was quite serious.

"Will you keep the name Fu, or shall you take your father's name now? Your children will carry what you choose."

"My esteemed emperor, my servants served me well through sickness and exile. I will keep the name Fu to remind my children that there is no greater honor than to serve this great nation."

The emperor did not give displeasure or pleasure. "So be it. Fu Xianning, return to your wife and to your home, and do not forget to return to your army when it is in need. But do not come to me again in your lifetime. You have disgraced your face with the blood spilled before this righteous throne."

In his heart, Xianning did not believe a throne built on blood and war could be in any way righteous. But he did not care if he never came to the palace again. It held no joy, no future. He bowed low, nearly shaking with relief that he would see his Jia Yi again. Both rings of jade and pearl were handed to him; he hated those pieces of jewelry and determined to destroy them. The emperor said he would no longer honor the decree that had been made to the Zhou's. The rings were merely trinkets now.

Xianning did not care. Power was apt to change and corrupt, and he needed no such things for his happiness. He numbly heard the old guard and the monk pardoned as well before the command was given, and he was finally released from the palace. He left the capital city and felt no regret to never see it again. He thundered home, galloping and keeping his record of five days in shortening the journey. But home held a horrible revelation.

He raced into an open gate, where no guards stood. He pulled up short in a courtyard where no servants worked. There was a deathly silence to the entire place. He leapt from his horse and ran through rooms, calling for Jia Yi and Yan Bin until his voice was hoarse.

Had the emperor's guards taken them to another place? Why had the emperor not mentioned it?

Had Zhou destroyed them all as his last wicked command? Even the cat could not be found.

For the first time in his life, Xianning felt broken. No wound, no injury had ever felt this painful. He went to his knees in despair, picking up a loose piece of silk he had crushed in his searching. It smelled like Jia Yi. Even in death, could Zhou have won? Could all have been in vain?

He did not know how long he sat there, numb and despairing. It finally occurred to him the light was nearly gone, and the blue shadows of dusk blanketed the room. He slowly stood; he would find her if he had to search the world over. Even if all he found was her remains, he would not stop until he knew.

He walked back outside and felt guilt at seeing the shaking horse that he had nearly killed on his ride. They had galloped at a furious rate. He rubbed the horse down, fed it food and water, and took a better look at the house. Nothing was disturbed, nothing was missing. They had not packed. But with everyone having left, was it prison that held them? And where?

Not one servant had been left behind, not one weapon lay idly about. No blood stained the tiles. The guards had not slain them here, but maybe they had been killed later? He sat by the fountain—with the spirit of Jia Yi hovering nearby. He could almost feel her. The memories in this empty house would drive him mad. He needed a plan. He just had to find out where to start looking. And he had to find a clue to make a plan. He needed to find one of his spies. But the usual method of sending the hawk with a message could no longer be used. He would have to find another way so they would know he had sent for them. He slowly stood up and looked at the sky. The moon was not up yet—but the stars were.

"I'm coming Jia Yi. If you still live, hold on. I'm coming."

UNTIL THE END OF TIME

Xianning stood on the temple roof, candle in hand. This was a known meeting place for him and his men. It wasn't his best method, but he had a saying that his soldiers and his spies knew: be the flame that starts the fire. Of course, what he meant was fight well and be the best. But the candle analogy would be noticed. He hoped.

It was late, and he worried whether or not his men were nearby or even still alive. The very faintest scratching sound was heard. He turned and saw one of his men, this one went by the name of Fox Eye, his most elusive spy. Xianning never knew his real name. Fox Eye stood before him, seemingly unarmed but doubtfully hiding numerous ways to kill about his person. This man was one of the best that Xianning had ever hired. The spy had seen the candle burning, faint and small but very real. He instinctively knew it was his leader.

They faced each other, Fox Eye's face was covered in scars; this man had traveled the continent for many years before returning to China. He worked for Xianning when he wasn't traveling, for he also did other jobs and Xianning never asked. He didn't want to know. But this one thing he did want to know, and Fox Eye would have an answer. He knew far more about even the most secret things in this country than Yan Bin.

"Where are they? Where is my wife?"

Fox Eye never blinked. "Zhou's men came for her."

"Zhou has been dead for six days now. What day was this?"

The man held up seven fingers. So Zhou had known Xianning was going to sneak into the capital and had already sent his men to take his treasure.

"Where to? Where is Yan Bin and the household?"

Yan Bin would not have let her be taken without a fight, even if all he had was his bare hands to wage war with. But the house had shown no signs of disturbance.

"Yan Bin went with her…and her maid." That was good. She had not been alone, at least for a while.

"Where?"

"First, a letter sent from you that fired every servant. Then the guards were dismissed as soon as they left."

"What? I sent no such message." "They knew it."

"But they still left?"

"The guards made sure they did. And it had the seal of emperor below your signature. The monk was discovered in your place, but I made sure he escaped a prison cell."

"Yes, the monk came and aided me at the capital. Where is she, Fox Eye? What happened to my wife?" He was as tense as he had ever been in battle.

"I trailed them for a few hours. They seemed to be heading for the capital. Then the carriage abruptly went over a cliff. It was sudden. I could not prevent it."

No. This could not be. "Where?"

"At a cliff's edge that meets the river below." He knew exactly where that was. The Yangtze River followed the road for many miles, until sheer cliffs had the road perched high above it. The Yangtze River had taken his wife and child.

"Why?" He wasn't sure why he said it out loud. Why? Because Zhou had determined to destroy him.

"I have been trying to find their trail…but nothing. I returned to find you and report the details.

And then I'm leaving." Xianning was quiet for a moment. Why would Fox Eye try to pick up a trail if they had…wait."

"They survived the fall?" "All three."

Ah, so the carriage driver had not. Likely Yan Bin had drowned him if the fall had not done the job.

"The current took them many miles and I lost sight, but all three were somehow still alive." The river was wild and swollen from rain. How a pregnant woman and an elderly lady had swam it, he couldn't fathom, even with Yan Bin to help.

"How far were you able to follow the river?" Xianning was strapping his cloak on tighter, preparing to leave the next moment.

"I will take you there."

Xianning was glad. He thought the man had said he was leaving, no doubt for another mission to another master. But he would at least take him as far as he could before Xianning was left to his own search. They moved with speed and precision, traveling until they reached the last point that Fox Eye had sighted them.

"They went around the bend there. The rocks do not allow them to get out, but not matter how I searched, I did not find a trail there or beyond it for many miles."

Perhaps they had drowned just past the next curve in the river. But Xianning would know for sure, even if he had to follow the river to the end.

"Thank you, Fox Eye. I will pay you well for this."

"No."

The refusal was so flat, Xianning glanced over. The scars on the man's face seemed deeper out here in the daylight.

"It was my last mission for you. I wish no payment, it was my honor." "You will not return then."

Silence was his answer.

"May the place your head rests bring you peace," Xianning said with a slight bow of deference.

He owed the man that much at least.

"I am leaving this business, I have somewhere to be and someone who needs me." Xianning knew his eyes showed surprise, though his trained face did not.

"I am glad, I hope you have many years to enjoy it."

The man gave the barest hint of a smile, then turned away and vanished into the rocks. Xianning was glad for him, and yet his stomach was churning in a way it never had before. For the first time he faced the reality that he himself had no one to go home to. If the worst had happened, if his Jia Yi was truly gone, life would be empty. How had a barbarian with gold hair done this to the youngest general in China? He didn't know. He only knew that, without her, he would be as lost as any sailor on a sea with no stars.

For months he searched every area along the riverbank for many miles. He knew, of course, that if they had survived that, Yan Bin would cover their trail for fear of enemies. But Yan Bin would also leave a sign behind for Xianning. How did he know this so certainly? He knew Yan Bin and that was enough.

He had lost track of how many days and weeks he had been at this when he saw an unmistakable sign. Two large rocks balanced on top of each other, and one small rock on top, along with three very small pebbles. It was so obvious, and yet if one did not know the meaning, it would seem just an odd thing. Rock sizes had meanings for Yan Bin, and they had often used this to communicate a direction when they had worked separately on missions. The first large rock on bottom was simply the base for the monument. The next rocks were directions. Large was north, medium was south, small was east, and smallest rock scales were for west. Pebbles were used for how many enemy troops. Each stood for one hundred men. But this time he knew that these three tiny pebbles meant Jia Yi, Yah Bin, and Qing Shan. All were still alive. He stared up at the sky, his relief momentarily stunning him to stillness. She was alive. He had to search northeast.

The dark of night for once did not slow his search. He walked relentlessly for days. He had not slept in so long, and he had hardly eaten, being purely driven by this drive to find Jia Yi. She was waiting for him; he just had to find where.

When he came over a rise, long-taught caution had him tucking down into tall grass. A small village was below. It seemed to have very few inhabitants, all busy working in fields or around the homes. He saw a few children and a woman holding a baby. It was not his Jia Yi though. With no sign of military stockades below, he approached the village at a steady walk. His sword clanged softy on his back, and his fingers toyed with his dagger hilt. One could never be too sure out here in the wilder stretches.

The people saw him coming, and they were scared. He knew he looked like a warrior coming to challenge, but he was too impatient to approach in a slower, more friendly demeanor.

An old man who appeared to be the village patriarch stood as Xianning approached, and he instinctively stepped toward him. He stopped before the older man and gave a respectful bow in answer to the one he received, but before he could speak, he heard shouting.

"Fu Xianning! General Xianning!"

Xianning knew that voice.

He turned about and saw Yan Bin dressed in farming attire coming toward Xianning at a dead run. When he reached Xianning, they embraced as long-lost brothers. Before Xianning could say a word, Yan Bin spoke.

"She is well, both Jia Yi and the baby. They are safe."

TO THE FINAL WORD

"Where?" Xianning asked, his jaw taunt with relief, but he had to see her for himself.

"Over the hill behind the village, there is a grove of trees. The baby was born too early, but they both are healthy now. She goes down there to the trees every evening and…" He hesitated, unsure how to say his thoughts. "She goes to think of you and pray for your safety, I believe."

Xianning grasped Yan Bin's shoulder, the words for thanks stuck in his throat. Then he released his best friend and strode rapidly toward where his heart was waiting.

He saw her among the trees, sitting on a carpet. Cherry blossom petals drifted down about her like a veil of flowers. She was looking toward the evening sun, her long hair wispy about her face. For a moment, he froze and allowed the wonder to reach his soul. She was alive, his own precious wife was alive. And she was more beautiful than he remembered.

Walking slowly to not startle her, he thought of all they had been through. Every fear, every tragedy, every event had been worth it.

She heard him walking, her ears could not be deceived. Hesitantly, she turned with a look of incredulity and stared at her approaching husband. For a moment, her face went white, then she was up and running toward him. Xianning was running now too. They collided in the middle, holding an embrace that even the breeze could not penetrate.

She was sobbing, and Xianning stroked her hair, whispering the same phrase repeatedly. "It's all over, Jia Yi, it's all over. We won."

When at last they pulled apart enough to look at one another, hands still holding tightly to each other, Jia Yi's face was full of questions, and Xianning began answering them. He told her everything that had happened, pausing to kiss away her tears when she cried with relief that Zhou was finally gone and would never be able to harm them again. She wanted to know so many things, and he could answer her unspoken questions. He could hear her thoughts as before; it was as if they had never been apart.

She was intrigued about how he had found them, giving her silent laugh when Xianning said, "I simply followed your heart."

At last, everything was said that needed to be, and he leaned in, holding her as if fearing she would vanish. Qing Shan walked along the edge of the grove. She seemed so much older now, but a cooing baby in her arms balanced age with innocence.

"Yes, I would love to meet our baby," Xianning said in answer to Jia Yi's hopeful eyes.

In another moment, he was holding a boy with jet black hair but with gray eyes that made him look like his mother. Xianning kissed the tiny forehead and reverently embraced his old nurse. Qing Shan's voice had a tremor to it. She had aged so much these last few weeks. But the woman had given her entire life to Fu Xianning, and he vowed her final days would be ones of rest and peace.

He turned back to Jia Yi. "What did you name the baby?" Her eyes sparkled, and she made a sword cutting motion.

"Perfect, he is named for Yan Bin. I would not have it any other way."

A few weeks later had them all safely transported back to his home. The missing servants had heard of the return and rushed back to beg for reemployment. Jia Yi did not turn anyone away. The village that had been under Xianning's protection for many years was grateful to have him back with them. But it was clear that it was Jia Yi that they loved. Gifts were sent for many days, and she was always gracious in her written thanks.

Qing Shan was now a companion of leisure; no duties were ever assigned to her, and Xianning and Jia Yi made it their highest duty to tend her in all things. Another small but wondrous moment occurred when the cat suddenly ambled back into the courtyard one morning. Jia Yi was overjoyed, and Xianning could not help the laugh that escaped him. Her happiness shone in her eyes; she felt like all the bad times were finally gone. He hoped for her sake they were.

After a few months, the whirlwind had quieted down. Xianning had found the old family guard and rewarded him handsomely, seeing that his days were peaceful ones. The priest would not accept any gifts but was glad to renew his teachings of medicine and remedies to Jia Yi.

Xianning and Jia Yi had resumed his work together. The army had heard rumors of the event, but the truth was long and messy. Xianning deemed only the barest most essential information be given to those closest to him, and for others he was content to leave uninformed.

Late one morning several generals came by for an unexpected visit to pay their respects for the new Fu family heir. Baby Fu Bin giggled and prattled in Jia Yi's arms, and the audience bowed respectfully. Xianning stood a step away from his little family. Yan Bin stood to the side, his firm military bearing only slack in the light of his eyes. Xianning felt an unrestrained smile slip onto his face. When the men had finished and left the compound, Jia Yi turned to her husband. A teasing smile was on her face.

"Yes, he is just as fine as the generals said." Xianning paused and laughed. "He does have my nose certainly."

She cuddled the baby to her, her eyes still alight with mischief and the joy of motherhood. Xianning reached out to stroke her face. No one anywhere could possibly be as happy as he.

Two days later a courier arrived with a message. He was announced in Xianning's office, both he and Jia Yi looking up with surprise. He was not one of the usual persons chosen for correspondence.

"It is from Muqali, my general." The man bowed with utmost reverence and no small amount of fear as he presented the missive. Xianning's face became as sharp as his blade. He stepped across the room and coolly retrieved it from the courier. The messenger was dismissed, and Xianning returned to his desk. He glanced at Jia Yi's worried face.

"I'll read it to you," he responded reassuringly.

Yan Bin walked in at that moment, having heard of the courier's peculiar delivery.

Xianning read aloud.

General Fu Xianning, my greetings I give and congratulate you. You have won. My infiltrator and spy is gone as is my youngest general. I can afford to lose him, Ilchidey's brashness would have been his undoing in the end. And losing Zhou was a setback, but he was a greedy conspirator.

My deepest regard for your abilities. You have fouled all of my plans, including the plan to undo you with the barbarian women. But her loyalty to you has earned my respect. I shall ever refer to her as the General's Wife, and you may consider it with my highest level of esteem. I shall spar with you in another life, Fu Xianning.

May the sun shine on you.

General Muqali

There was a moment of stunned silence, then Jia Yi was standing on one side of Xianning and Yan Bin was standing on the other.

"You beat Muqali," Yan Bin said in awe, and Jia Yi squeezed her husband's large hand in her tiny one. Yan Bin stepped out to be alone in his marveling, and Xianning turned to Jia Yi.

He pulled her forward and smiled. "I love the name, the General's Wife. It suits you." Jia Yi smiled back and kissed him.

"Yes, I think I shall always refer to you by that title. I reached the epitome of good fortune the day you became my bride."

And they lived happily for the rest of their days.

FROM THE AUTHOR

Thank you for reading *The General's Wife* and accompanying me on this journey. I hope you have enjoyed this little mystery/romance. This story roughly begins around 1206, though it is not meant to be a historical tale—more of a "what could have happened." I was inspired by tales of Marco Polo, Genghis Khan, and other world events from the medieval period. My imagination likes to muse over the past and, though this tale is pure fiction, the endeavor was to honor the men and women who made history, especially those whose names are unknown. History is said to be told by the victors, but history is made by the courageous. No matter how small a part you think you play in the world, you are never insignificant. This story is for them and for you.

www.ingramcontent.com/pod-product-compliance
Lightning Source LLC
LaVergne TN
LVHW041625070526
838199LV00052B/3248